FALSE CONFESSIONS, FALSE ALARMS:

SHORT STORIES (AND ONE SHORT PLAY)

Jeremy Puma

ISBN: 0615786790
ISBN-13: 978-0615786797

DEDICATION

Dedicated to Nicholas Cooper Puma, who is far too young to be reading such filth!

CONTENTS

ACKNOWLEDGMENTS

Many and continuous thanks to the contributors who made the publication of this title possible: Miguel Conner, Spence Fothergill, Charles Hertenstein, Paul Hillman, David Morgan, Heather Nolting, Ronnie and Marilyn O'Daniell, Gareth Pashley, John Plummer, Matthew Smith and Robert Wood.

1. Delivery

Jean wrinkled his nose and rustled the newspaper. "Now they're asking us to voluntarily dispose of them in any way possible. They've run out of room at the animal shelters."

"Horrible!" remarked Linda, over her shoulder from the kitchen. She reached down and retrieved a two pound bag of cat food from under the counter. Placing it on the table, she turned back to the counter and stood for a moment, knowing what she needed next but taking a second to think of where it was, waving her hands absently through the air. "How many are we up to now?"

"Seven," replied Jean, who had put down the paper and stood in the doorway to the kitchen, leaning against the jamb. "Not counting Frederick. The latest arrived this morning. I think it's a female, but I don't know where it's run off to."

"It'll be here soon enough. Do you know where the cat dish is?"

"Hm," he replied, crossing to the dishwashing machine. He opened it and extracted a small plastic bowl with 'Freddy' printed on the side in black paw- print letters. Handing her the dish, he grabbed a knife and proceeded to hack at the bag of cat food.

Linda paused, inspecting the cat dish, and sighed. "This isn't big enough."

"You're right," he said. "It was fine when we just had Frederick, but I think we may need a bigger one. I wonder if we'll be able to find a bigger dish anywhere. I'll bet the pet stores are sold out."

"Probably," she replied. "Well, we can't use that little thing, unless we want to feed them in shifts, and that's a pain. Do we have anything else that would do? A big pot? A container of some kind?"

Jean returned to the dishwasher. "These are all dirty," he said, "and there's nothing big enough even if they were clean."

Frustrated, Linda began slamming through the kitchen cabinets. "Dammit, we need some bigger containers."

"Why? We didn't have any need for larger containers. It's not like we have vast amounts of leftovers that require storage."

"It's just something we should have around the house. Large containers are like the guest towels of kitchen supplies. You should always have a bunch of containers. Even if you never use them, at least you'll know they're there." She crashed a cabinet door closed, and the glassware inside trembled and shook. With pronounced steps, she pulled the junk drawer out of the cabinet, took a moment to extract it, to lift the plastic wheels out of their tracks and maneuver the drawer past the tabs that held it in place. She set it on the table, where the mounds of half- charged batteries and unused paper clips sat and rattled until she lifted it again, dumping its contents into a plastic bag.

"What are you doing?" asked Jean, as she proceeded to grab the now open bag of cat food and fill the drawer.

"We have to feed them in something. We can't just pour food all over the floor."

Jean ran his hand over her back. "Darling, you're taking this too hard. Think of Matthew! He's been getting two a day. He's up to fourteen. Fourteen cats, delivered fresh to his door every morning."

"It's sick," she shouted. She popped the drawer full of cat food onto the floor next to three bowls of water, and opened the washroom door. Seven cats, two black and whites, a calico, an orange striped, two gray, and a Siamese, trotted expectantly into the kitchen and greedily began devouring the food. "Where's the new one?"

"Upstairs, I think," said Jean. "You want me to go look?" As if on cue, a tiny brown kitten crawled through his legs like a wingless insect and made its way to the drawer, where the other cats growled until it was able to push itself between two of them. With an exploratory pounce, it hefted itself up the side of the drawer, over, and into the food, where it stood, legs akimbo, crunching the fishy brown nuggets.

"It is cute, I'll give it that," said Linda, taking out the dishwashing liquid and filling the soap container in the dishwasher. "I can't remember ever having seen a pure brown cat before." She closed the machine and turned it on, the humming and churning of water running through it quickly rising to a crescendo. "So," she said, filling a glass with water, "you still don't want to name any of them?"

"I just think it'd be a bad idea, don't you? You never know how long this is going to keep going on, how many other mornings a new meow will be added to the rest of the 'Chorus' in there. The Government is already asking that we put them down at home, voluntarily, as a kind of warning to the terrorists. If this keeps up, we'll eventually be required to have them all killed, put to sleep. We don't want to get too attached to them."

"But you've already named the collective: 'The Greek Chorus.'" With a prrp, the newest member of the group hopped out of the drawer and began busily licking itself clean between Jean's feet. Frederick, a fat black and white with green eyes and a toothy grin, pranced over to Linda, stretched with front legs out and rear in, and began asking for attention. She picked the cat up with a whoof, remembering the feel of warmth and fuzz of his kitten-hood and wondering when he got so big. "I'd just like to refer to them in some way other than 'brown cat,' or, 'hey you,' or . . . you know. I guess I've lived with Frederick for so long they all seem like people to me."

"Well, darling, they're not. And you can't think of them that way. If we get too attached, we'll end up regretting it. When the Government gives the okay to keep them, then we'll discuss names for any that we decide to take on."

"That's another thing," she said, setting Frederick down on the table, where he perched rolled- over, balanced on his spine, feet in the air. "If they do make that announcement, are we going to keep all eight cats?"

Jean reached down quickly, scruffed the kitten, lifted it to eye level, and replied. "Eight? Dear, if they don't make that announcement soon, it'll be far more than eight. Ah, a girl. I was right, I can tell." He set the kitten gently to the floor, gave it a swift pat on the rear. "I don't think it's a possibility, Lin. We eventually want to have room for children, right?"

Glumly, she threw away the empty cat food bag and set about scratching each one on its head.

***

"It's a violation!" shouted Matthew. He and Jean sat over a

pitcher of urine colored beer in the bottom floor restaurant of their office building, on a lunch break. "It's a violation of personal space." He waved to the waitress, indicated an ashtray, which she carted over nonchalantly.

"It's a brilliant act of terrorism," replied Jean, nodding his head agreeably. "Nobody gets hurt, physically. It plays upon humanity's inherent kindness. And, I hate to say, it certainly helped with the stray cat population problem this City has. Or, had."

Matthew twisted the end of his necktie and moaned. "You may think it's brilliant, my friend, but you're getting it easy. You only find one new cat at your front door every morning. I've found two, every single morning so far for the past eight days. That's sixteen cats I have, if you can't do the math! You know how much I've spent on cat food alone? And the litter box— it has to be emptied, you know, it has to be emptied constantly! And speaking of empty, all the pet stores are empty: cleaned out by people who may be getting more than me!"

Jean couldn't help but laugh. "Aren't you going to have them destroyed?"

"Of course, of course." He poured himself another glass of beer from the pitcher. "It's just that I don't want to do it myself, you know? Since all the veterinarians are so backed up... I've never killed something before, and..."

"No, I understand," said Jean. "That's part of the reason Linda and I are waiting. That and... well, Lin thinks that Frederick likes the company. I think she may want to keep one, maybe two of them."

"More like nine or ten, when all is said and done," said Matthew, taking a gulp and lighting a cigarette. "I mean, how are they doing it? They must have hundreds of operatives, thousands, to deliver all of those baskets and all of those cats to so many people every night. There can't be that many stray cats in this City alone. They probably employ 'cat collectors' in every City in the area. It's a violation, I tell you! And thanks to them I have a closet full of baskets and sixteen cats."

"What I want to know," said Jean, "is how they chose their targets. And why. Not everyone is getting cats, after all. Just enough people to throw the local animal care industry into a panic."

Matthew leaned in close over the table, holding onto the pitcher so as not to accidentally tip it over. "That reminds me," he said, whispering, looking carefully left and right. "You know Sherman, from Propaganda?"

"Yeah. I went to college with him, but we never really talked."

"Well, I heard that he's not getting any cats, right? So the other day, he gets a call at work from the cops." He lifted his eyebrows, knowingly.

"They think he's in on it?"

"Heh. Get this: not only do they think he's in on it, but they think everyone who doesn't get cats is in it. So they're calling everyone who didn't report getting cats, calling them every day, and each person has to let the police know where they were at, you know, at delivery time." He sat back, smug, eyes wide open and head nodding up and down.

"I think that's paranoid bullshit," Jean spat. "Where are we, Nazi Germany, that we have to explain where we were every night between three and five AM? You'd think that a group with such obvious talent for planning would have included a few of their own members in the delivery scheme, to throw off the cops."

Matthew jabbed with his finger at invisible plot points in

the air. "But the cops think, that the group thought, that they'd think that, so they didn't actually deliver any cats to any of their own operatives, to throw the cops off, thinking that the police would be too stupid to catch on. So the cops really think that the people who aren't having cats delivered are the terrorist group."

"Where'd you hear this confusing gobbledegook?" He laughed. "I simply don't believe it. The cops have too much to do; they can't call everyone who doesn't get cats delivered, every day. That's far too many people to call."

"You'd think so, eh?" replied Matthew, leaning in again, but not as closely. "But here's something else I've heard. Apparently, some people think that there is no terrorist group."

Jean smirked incredulously. "What? Now that's going too far. It's ridiculous. No terrorist group? But there was a letter, a manifesto. It was printed in all the papers."

"I know, I know. But the people who ascribe to this theory think it's the Government that's delivering the cats, and that the Government also wrote the 'Idealism Manifesto.' They think the Government— "

"Government, Government, Government! Alright, already. Everything that goes wrong is traceable to the Government, for these people. UFOs, Torreo's assassination, and now the cat deliveries, too."

"Yes, yes, I agree. There's no conspiracy." He gulped down the rest of his beer. "Let's forget I even brought it up. Listen, Jean. I know that Linda loves cats. Perhaps you could take a few off of my hands for me? You only have eight, nine including Frederick. I have sixteen. Come on, man; I'm a bachelor. You were there once. Do you know, can you imagine bringing a date home to the mewlings and odor of sixteen cats? It's killing my love life!"

"Hah! My friend, I sympathize with your conundrum, but where's the fine line between the number we could take from you and the number you'd be stuck with when the next two were delivered? Say we took five of your sixteen. You'd still have eleven, and then two more the next day would be thirteen. And if we took any more, we'd have more than you, which wouldn't be proper, I'm sure you'd agree. I'm afraid we can't take on any more than we already have. If you don't want all those cats around, you'll have to put them down, I'm afraid."

Matthew groaned. "You're right, of course," he said, rising and throwing a pair of fives onto the table. "When will it stop, Jean? These terrorists, if there really are any, they're making killers of us all. You realize that, don't you? It'll soon get to a point where we'll have to begin killing cats every single day, every single one of us."

"Hm, I hadn't looked at it that way," Jean replied, pushing away the four or five cats that curled around his legs like stoles and pushing his chair back with a loud screech that scattered the felines. "Brilliant, of course. Maybe they'll run out of cats?" "I hope they do," agreed Matthew. "I really hope they do."

***

At the end of the second week, Jean and Linda were spending more on food for the cats than on food for themselves. Amidst the yowlings and crashes of furred bodies as the creatures bounded through the house, Linda tried to finish the magazine she'd bought before the cats started arriving, a magazine that she'd just now been able to pick up. Jean, napping upstairs, had sparked a long and sullen disagreement, when he announced that his friend Matthew now killed five cats a day, and would soon be rid of them all, and he thought it was high time they followed suit. Linda, on the other hand, despised the idea of killing so many innocent creatures, thrown into a situation that they couldn't control. She'd rather wait, she told him, until the animal clinics were no longer backlogged and could do it for them.

She gazed softly at Frederick, spread across the top of the television set, absorbing the modicum of heat it broadcast with the latest Government bulletin on Idealist activity. How confused he must be, she thought to herself, with all of this new company. But he doesn't act like it; he's always been so personable. It's lucky for us that all of these cats seem to like one another, just one of the many perplexing behaviors of the new additions to the household. Over the magazine, she noticed that Carmine had Little Max pinned down, coating the kitten with a layer of licks. Carmine must've lost her own litter, thought Linda.

In the den, the phone rang. Linda tossed the magazine aside, frustrated, and growled. She skipped into the den and caught the phone on the fourth ring. "Hello?"

"Lin? Hi, it's Mom!"

"Hi, Mom! How was Brazil?" Her Mother had just returned from a month long trip to the tropics that she'd won in a contest.

"Oh, it was, you know. Dirty. But fun. We had fun. Your father has a tan; you should see him!"

"That's nice. You'll have to tell me all about it."

"But Lin, we're more curious about you. We've heard about the cats. Are you on... you know, are you having cats brought to you?"

Linda sighed and scattered a look at the five cats perched above the main bookshelf. "Yeah, Mom. We've been getting them. We have fifteen now, counting Freddie."

"These people are insane," replied her mother, despondently. "I told you and Jean not to move into the City. If something like that happened out here, well, we'd simply put them down."

"Yeah, well, it's not that easy here, Mother. The animal clinics are backed up, so we just have to take care of them for a while, until they— "

Jean's voice entered the den from the living room. "Hon? You may want to see this."

"Oh, can you hang on a minute, Mom? Jean wants to show me something. Be right back." She set the phone down next to Bruce, an orange tabby who had set up temporary residence on the desk next to the computer.

Jean, awake in the living room dressed in his robe, had turned up the volume of the television, on which a plasticene, android- like newscaster stood in front of St. Benedict's Hospital, downtown. "This may be the answer to our problem," he said in a whisper.

On the screen, the reporter swiveled towards the camera as if her legs had been replaced by a unicycle. "Again, if you're just tuning in, we are now receiving news on the first death in what is being called the most nefarious act of terrorism in this City's history. Earlier today, Lt. Gary Argent of the City Police Force, checked himself into St. Benedict's complaining of what was later diagnosed as an allergic reaction to cat dander. According to hospital spokesperson Emily Goldberg, Mr. Argent died approximately one hour ago due to an allergy related condition. We spoke with Mr. Argent's sister, who had this to say."

The shot cut to a dark, dirty, cat- filled apartment decorated with Hindu wall hangings. A pasty woman, pimple- covered face and long, stringy hair pulled back into a ponytail spoke to the camera through tears. "I can't believe it. Just this morning, he was fine, and then he started wheezing after breakfast. I told him to go to the doctors. It's these cats. I hope the terrorists are happy. My brother served this City for ten years, and this is what he gets as payment. It's sick!"

The reported reappeared. "Lt. Argent was forty one years old and is survived by his wife, his sister, and two brothers. Authorities are expected to make an official statement from City Hall in just a moment."

Linda backtracked to the phone. "Sorry, Mom, I have to go. There's some important news coming in." "Okay, hon. I'll send you an e- mail about the trip. Now don't get too frustrated, and don't be afraid to do what you have to do. Okay?"

"Sure, Mom. Love you."

"Love you too. Bye, dear!"

Jean crouched in front of the television, patting a grey which she called Mikey. The cat purred its way through his legs and over his knees. The camera cut to a large, white auditorium, filled with cameras and suited reporters. After a moment, the Mayor and the Chief of Police stepped behind a green podium, on the front of which floated a holographic image of the City Seal. The Mayor began: "Ladies and gentlemen, esteemed members of the press, we have asked you all here today to release an official statement on the cat problem. I will now turn the microphone over to Police Chief Sandra Pollack, who will explain the new policy. Please hold all questions until she is done speaking. Thank you."

Police Chief Pollack stepped to the podium, brushed a lock of brown hair out of her eyes, blankly stared at the gathered assemblage of reporters and VIPs. "Thank you, Mr. Mayor. As you all know by now, earlier today, the first casualty of the cat delivery problem was reported by St. Benedict's Hospital. The victim, Lieutenant Gary Argent, faithfully served and protected the people of this City for ten years as an officer of the law. Unfortunately, the tragedy doesn't stop there. It is my regretful duty to inform you that at approximately six thirty- five this evening, a Mrs. Olga Afferty, 65, passed away at City General, also of an allergic reaction to the fourteen cats which had been delivered to her house for the past two weeks." The auditorium broke into an uproar of mumbles and whispers.

"Great," muttered Jean. "A cop and an old woman."

Pollack continued once the wave of sound subsided. "In light of these circumstances, the Mayor and I have been in a meeting for the last half hour with members of the National Advisory Committee on Terrorism, and have come to the conclusion that swift and immediate action must be taken to prevent further deaths.

"The resulting policy will be implemented as follows. The Mayor has called the National Guard, who will be arriving in the City in approximately two hours. We are instituting a curfew beginning at seven PM and ending at seven AM for all residents of the City, until further notice. Any resident caught out of doors between these hours will be arrested, unless on official or job-related business. "When the National Guard arrives, they will be setting up Feline Disposal Units in each neighborhood. Disposal of excess felines will be mandatory, and enforced. Until this matter is resolved and the terrorists have been captured, the City will officially be in a state of martial law." More muttering. Linda's hand rose to her mouth as she looked from oblivious cat to oblivious cat. Jean stood and placed his arm around his wife.

"Now," continued the Police Chief. "Are there any questions? Yes, you," she said, pointing to a reporter in the third row.

He stood, adjusted his hat, and started scratching on his notepad as he spoke. "Yes, Steve Singleton, News- Tribune. Madame Police Chief, doesn't this policy seem a little excessive? I mean, we are just talking about cats here. Is martial law really necessary?"

"We don't feel that it's excessive," answered Pollack. "After discussing the matter with NACT, we feel that it's important that all citizens cooperate in showing these Idealists that we will not be intimidated by their schemes. Swift, direct action must be taken to avoid more cat related deaths. Next? You."

"Megan Forbes, WKNT. Madame Police Chief, how will the Police Department work with the National Guard to dispose of all of the cats?"

"Yes, as I mentioned, each neighborhood will have a National Guard post stationed in a central location. Guardsmen will be surveying each household to determine the number of excess cats needing disposal. All citizens will be required to report the exact number of extra cats residing in their home, and then deliver those cats to the post by curfew each night, where they will be destroyed. Citizens who do not have cats delivered are exempt from reporting, of course, but will still be required to abide by the curfew. Again, anyone who does not comply with the policy will be subject to a— "

Linda threw her magazine at the television, somehow striking the power switch, and the Police Chief disappeared into a rectangle of dark grey.

"What did you do that for?" asked Jean. "I wanted to see the rest of that."

"I don't want anything to do with the whole affair. Look at them!" She motioned to the animals, who sat around the room in various states of 'cat.' Some cleaned themselves with long, pink tongues; some played with bits of dust or one another's tails; some slept the long sleep of cats, blissful, dreaming perhaps of the odor of fish, or of bringing down zebras in the savannah. "They have no idea. They're totally innocent, totally innocent of anything at all. They're just animals! And tomorrow they could all be dead, that's what the City is telling us." Jean wrapped his arms around his trembling wife, stroked her dark hair as if it sat on a feline's back. "Linda, we have to turn them over to the guardsmen. If we don't, then they'll— "

"Then they'll what? Arrest us? Is that what they'll do?"

"I don't know. But whatever it is they plan to do, it's not worth it. It's not worth risking your life, or your freedom, over the lives of a few stray cats."

She pushed him away towards the den. "But I can't! I can't turn these cats over to the fucking National Guard to be killed."

Jean shivered, never having heard his wife use profanity before. "But Linda, that's what's going to happen. That's the situation. There is no moral right or wrong here. Not one that can be applied, anyhow. The facts are there: the cats exist. There are too many of them. The City wants to get rid of them, so they bring in the National Guard to get rid of them quickly and efficiently. Think of it this way: everyone is being inconvenienced by the cats, including us. Just the other day you were mentioning how annoying it was that we didn't have a container big enough for cat food, and how expensive it's getting— "

"Yes, but— "

"Let me finish. How expensive it's getting... darling, we can barely afford to take care of one cat, much less fourteen. But in a few days, we won't have to worry about it anymore. It'll all be taken care of, the curfew will end, and once they start killing the cats, don't you think they'll stop being delivered? No organization can exist by knowingly sending so many innocent animals to their deaths. They'll stop sending them."

"And if they don't? What if it just keeps up? What if this is life, from now on: wake up, take in the new cat, feed it, send a report to the Guardsmen who come over, every night, at seven, pick up the cat, kill it. Could you do it? Could you?"

Two of the cats, tails in the air, whiskers aglow, purred their way to where the couple stood, silently, looking at one another, she dreadfully, he expectantly. Soon the other cats joined the first two, surrounded the motionless couple, giants in a moving sea of fur and tail, orange and black and white and brown, long and short hair, Siamese, Persian, Alley, and Tabby. Behind them all sat Frederick, bolt upright on the television set, tail behind him parallel to his spine, the only cat in the room, thought Linda, that could be sure of its impending safety.

***

When Jean came home from work the next evening, Linda already had dinner prepared. "I made dinner tonight," she said. "I figured you'd be tired."

"This is a pleasant surprise," he replied, delivering a peck to her cheek. He took off his jacket and tossed it onto the hair covered couch. "Amazing, isn't it," he said, "how much cats shed. But I see you did the right thing. Even the new one is gone." To his pleasant surprise, the only cat in the living room was Frederick, who curled himself into a ball on the couch. The television news flashed across the screen, amusement park sized lines of people with light blue, Government issue cat carriers, each of which had multiple tails projecting from the mesh, images of green trucks filled with cats, then a diagram of the chemicals used to painlessly put the felines to sleep. With a murp, Frederick pounced off of the couch and onto Jean's shoes. He lifted the heavy cat into his arms. "There you are, big boy. How's it feel finally having the house to yourself again, eh? He's the master of his domain, once again."

Linda spooned a tuna and pea casserole out of a dish and onto two plates. "How was your day?" she asked.

"Oh, long and boring. The office talk was all the news from last night, of course. Everyone has their cat, you know? I tell you, most people seem genuinely relieved that the cats are gone. Sheesh, get this. You know how Matthew's been disposing of them himself for the past few days? Apparently he had a breakdown yesterday. Having to kill all of those cats himself, it was just too much for him to take."

"I can imagine," she replied.

"Of course, the Government is calling it another 'cat related psychosis,' or whatever. Did you hear that six more people are in the hospital for allergies? And there's a case of cat scratch fever." He took his seat at the table, picked up his fork as she sat across from him. "So what happened today with the Guard? I have to say, you look okay. I thought for sure you'd be going crazy."

"I told them that we didn't have any cats delivered," she announced, nonchalantly.

Jean dropped his fork. "You what?!"

"I told the guardsman that we didn't have any cats. They weren't searching the houses or anything. He was a rather polite young man, and I told him there weren't any here."

"But we've already reported that there are some here!"

"I'm not an idiot, Jean. I told him we disposed of them ourselves."

He pushed his chair back across the linoleum and stood, violently. "Where are they? Where are the cats?" Determined, he tossed open the washroom door. "Where are they? Here, kitty kitty kitty. Here, kitty kitty kitty!"

Linda continued eating. "They're upstairs," she said over a mouthful of casserole. "They're in the bedroom."

"Oh, great," he replied, shouting and pacing. "This is wonderful. Now what? We're breaking the law. You think they won't find out? You think they don't have ways of telling whether or not you're lying?"

With a sigh, she stood, placed her hands on Jean's shoulder. "Calm down. I have a plan. I thought this out completely."

"Oh, she has a plan," he grumbled. "Listen, this plan had better be good, or else I will have to kill all of those cats. And I will, don't you doubt it for a minute. I'll wring every single one of their necks. I don't care what their names are."

"Calm the fuck down!" she yelled. "Calm down and I'll explain it to you. Sit down, eat dinner. I cooked. Everything is okay."

He breathed, in, out, slipped out of his shoes for lack of a better idea, crossed to his chair and sat down, tapped his fork on the table twice. "Okay."

"You sure? Are you going to calmly listen to me?"

"Yes."

"All right then. Here's the deal. Tomorrow, I'm going to get up early and load the cats into the car. Then I'm going to drive to Mother's, in the hills. Then I unload the cats. Mom says she can find good homes for all of them. The farms out there always need cats, to get rid of mice."

"But I need the car for work."

"Then you can call in sick tomorrow. After all, someone needs to be here to talk to the guardsman when he comes by."

"And that's it? That's your plan? What about the roadblocks, Linda?"

"I don't know." She massaged her temples. "I'm not sure. All I know is that I can't consign all of those cats to death. I can't do it, Jean."

Wordlessly, he rose, scraped his casserole into the garbage disposal, and left the kitchen.

"Where are you going?" she asked.

"The den," he answered through the door. "I'm going to call the National Guard post, tell them there's been a mistake, that you hadn't taken your medication or something." She leapt up, ran after him, pushed Frederick aside with her leg as the cat tried to get underfoot. Jean stood over the desk, phone at his ear, "yes, hi, my name is Jean— " With a hopscotch- sized lurch, Linda slammed her index finger onto the phone's cradle, hanging up. He slammed the mouthpiece into the desk, bang bang bang. "Damn it all, Lin! You're being ridiculous!"

"I'm not the one trying to kill things, here, all right?!"

"But you're going to... we're going to go to god- knows-where because of this! I need you to be here, Linda. We're just starting to adjust to it here! We're just trying to— "

A vast and hollow pound from the living room, followed by a crashing, splintering, bang interrupted him. "Mr. and Mrs. LeMans? Mr. and Mrs. LeMans? We know you're here; the car is here." The voice, amplified by a megaphone, preceded a clopping march which emanated from the room like tentacles and spread throughout their house, over their heads, under their feet, one of the tendrils swinging open the door to the den, admitting a green man, a soldier.

"A Guardsman," whispered Jean, dropping the phone.

"Sir, they're here," shouted the guardsman, training a rifle at them.

"There's one," came the same voice as before, unamplified. "Get that one. Where? Upstairs? Fine, fine."

A moment later, a man, who must be the officer, thought Linda, opened the den door, stood, legs slightly apart, hands crossed behind his back. "Good evening, Mr. and Mrs. LeMans. Yes, we've come for the cats."

"They knew," said Linda, clutching for Jean.

"Yes, we knew," said the officer. "We've got the whole City covered in cameras. Word of advice, Mrs. LeMans? Next time you're trying to hide that many cats in a room, you may want to close the blinds."

"Shit," said Jean. "You didn't close the blinds," and he clutched her, tightly.

"What's going to happen to us?" she asked.

"First, you'll come with us," he sighed, "to the nearest Feline Disposal Unit, where you will personally put down every single one of these cats. Then, Cat— Shelterers, you will be taken to a dark hole somewhere, and tossed into it for a long while. Then you will be tried for treason and crimes against man and animal, and then you will be put back into the dark hole for a very, very long time."

Another guardsman pushed his way into the room, light— blue carrier full of cat in hand, hoisted to eye level; it looked as though the cat carrier replaced his head. "Sir," he said through the barrier of fur, "we've found them all, sir."

"Good, Lieutenant Argent. Take them to the truck."

"Yes, sir. To the truck!" he shouted, turning about, swinging the carrier down and back and into the den for a split second, into the den just long enough for Linda and Jean to see Frederick's wide, green eyes, meow, behind the mesh of blue.

"Shall we go?" asked the officer.

2. Directions

Right now, a tiny, yellowed triangle of paper with faint traces of blue lines, torn out of an archaic collection of collections of words that he attempted, in college, to pass as poetry, holds the immediate position as the most important thing in Wester's life, and he can't find it. He and Liz have given the third degree to every inanimate object in the car, have emptied the gluttonous recess of glove compartment three times, have risked manual exploration of the dark, cluttered abysses under the seats, have pulled to the side of the road at a vacant and forlorn intersection that would have, no doubt, been teeming with traffic during rush- hour and, surrounded by drops of rain, unpacked each individual piece of the tapir- skin luggage Liz's father had given them three years ago, all to no avail. They simply can't find the directions.

"Why'd you write it on something so small?" asks Liz from the driver's seat, as Wester stands in the intersection, alternately peering up at the road signs and down at a map of the city.

"I was digging through a box of old stuff when they called me. It was the only thing handy at the time."

"You could've transferred it to something more manageable, couldn't you?"

Wester scoffs. "Like what? Another piece of paper? We'd just have lost that, too. This trip wasn't exactly something that I had a lot of time to plan for, you'll remember."

"Yeah, every time I reach for the damn phone you left on the dresser that you wouldn't go back for. Wouldn't the GPS be nice right about now?" Liz shrugs, leans on the steering wheel and smoothes her ruffled brown skirt, the same one she's been wearing for the past twelve hours. "I don't see why I had to come to this fucking thing anyway. Let's just get a room somewhere and look in the morning. You can drive around the city all day. We can get a red pen and fill in the streets as we go, so we won't hit the same place twice." She yawns, stretches. "Why is it that sitting in the same seat for twelve hours can be so tiring?"

Wester has been struggling to fold the map, trying to match the grooves where the fold lines streak across the image of the city, quite unsuccessfully. "I remember that my dad used to have a subscription to this nature magazine," he says, to nobody in particular, because Liz stopped listening. "It'd have these maps of Africa, Europe, Australia, with plastic overlays showing bird distribution in blues and purples, ecosystems in greens and browns, and topography in off— centered circles and dotted lines. I used to wonder whether the cosmonauts could see the world as it was on these maps, as pastel and abstract regions of geography marked by optical and linear concept." Frustrated, he finally decides that map folding is based on faulty human social convention, and that it's completely unnecessary to return the map to its original shape and size. "Those maps went a long way in helping me to decide what I wanted to do with my life." He wads it up and tosses it through the car window, like an executive who thinks that his ability to throw paper away means he can play basketball. "I couldn't fold those maps, either."

"I've heard about the maps," she grumbles. "Too bad you couldn't get one that has the Convention Center on it. When's that one from, Nineteen Sixty- Two? Isn't that an ad for the World's Fair? I should've stayed at home with the cats."

Wester skips over the puddles in the street, opens the passenger- side door and sits. He takes Liz's hand, runs his thumb over her smooth fingers with their silver and turquoise rings. "Look, I told you, I wanted you to come along because... well, because it's important to me, that's all. I want to be with you. And getting a room someplace else would be silly and expensive. We already have one booked across from the Convention Center. It's paid for, so I can't afford to pay for another. Besides that, it's urgent that I get to the nine o'clock meeting. What time is it?"

She sighs, reaches into her purse, which sits between the two front seats, balancing delicately on the emergency break, and exhumes a cheap, digital quartz watch. "It's almost five. Look, if we're not going to get a room someplace soon, then you drive, or we stop someplace where I can get coffee. No way can I keep going at this rate." She pulls her sweater over her head, tosses it into the back seat.

"I don't mind driving," he mutters, having driven for the last three hours due to her fear of maneuvering down any street with more than five cars. Liz sees something in Wester's face which belies his reticence to continue driving. With a realization that he means so well, he always means so well and that's one of his traits that makes her crazy and irritable sometimes, she closes her door and turns the key, starting the engine, which, cold and wet, makes a noise not unlike the sound of a screaming mouse. "I'm sorry, hon," she says to him. "I'm just really beat. I know how important this meeting is for you. Let's just drive around for a little while and see if we can find someplace to ask directions. These people have to know where their Convention Center is, right?"

He smiles, glad she's acquiesced, not only because he won't have to drive, but also because when he squeaked into the seat a minute ago, he began to worry that bringing her along may not have been the best idea after all. But now the car is rolling, slowly at first, but then more steadily, through the intersection after stopping for a traffic light that blinks yellow, red, yellow, red. Banana, tomato, thinks Wester, banana, tomato. No more rain, at least— the windshield wipers end after a brief jaunt back and forth over the glass. He shuffles his jacket off of his shoulders and leans back. Next comes the unsettling experience of waking up in a car without knowing for how long he's been out. The radio churning out some local news broadcast seems to display its wares on a lower sonic register than he's used to, perhaps altered by the alpha waves that slowly recede into his brain. "How long have I been asleep?" he asks.

"You were asleep?" replies Liz. "I didn't notice. It can't have been more than ten minutes or so. I've only been driving for about fifteen."

"I didn't notice either. Where are we?" Slightly refreshed by the nap, Wester sits up and curls his legs beneath him, tries to ignore the cracks and tenses and knots that scurry up and down his back like tiny Scandinavian trolls searching for acorns. He rolls down the window low enough to ventilate the smoke from a cigarette without freezing the air in the car, the newscaster's low tones now interrupted by a rushing whir and the smell of a city's industrial area.

"Gimme one of those," says Liz, holding out her hand for a smoke. "I don't know where we are. Maybe from the signs... Georgetown? Looks like a bunch of factories and warehouses. What do they make around here?"

"Nothing, I think. These look like train yards on the left, maybe storage facilities? I dunno. See anybody around yet?"

"Not a soul. It's like a ghost town— a huge, industrial ghost town, with trains. Except no trains."

Wester looked behind them. "No, there's one moving, back towards all those skyscrapers. Shouldn't we be able to see the Space Needle from here? I don't know. I can see the train lights crawling along. Unless it's one of those angler fish from the Marianas Trench, with the bioluminous globe on its head, and no eyes."

"Here to lure unsuspecting cars into its gaping maw?" She chuckles, turns left, away from the rails, flips the radio station to some sort of late night jazz. "Well, there are people in the radio station, that's comforting. We could always call in a request for directions."

"Yeah, if we can find a phone." Grey, ponderous masses loom up around them, looking less like warehouses than like giant, square, concrete whales on an abandoned beach. "Back east, this'd be a bad neighborhood. Around here, there's nothing to steal. Look, not even any cars." It's true; they don't see a single auto around them, and are subject to a feeling of disturbing wonder rather like the feeling one gets when one finds a working clock on a lonely mountain trail.

"Look!" shouts Liz. "Is that a person?" She slows, points to the left where, in the slight glow of the headlights, the shadows have enlisted a human figure shambling just ahead. "Should I ask him for directions?"

"I don't see another option," says Wester, sitting up further and rolling up his window.

As the car inches forward, the outline becomes clearer, and it's a bundled man, elderly, with gray, mottled scarf and knit cap, red, like someone's donation to a homeless charity come to life and struggling to escape. On his shoulder, he carries a hulking, unwieldy rectangle, a sign, unreadable, attached to a mop handle. "A sign?" wonders Wester. "Hmm."

"Bad sign," Liz replies. "No pun intended. Should we really ask directions from a sign- carrier?"

Wester glances at the dashboard. "We don't really have a choice. We're running low."

"Okay, no conversation though. We ask him where the nearest gas station is, and then we're off. And if he starts some tirade about Jesus or something, we're out of here."

"Sounds fine. Let's just get it over with." She pulls the car next to the man, who stops, stares. As he turns to face the car, Wester and Liz see that he's wearing a white suit surmounted by an old- fashioned butterfly bow tie, he looks like a plantation owner, or a Nineteenth Century aristocrat. The letters have abandoned the front of his sign; the earlier rainstorm forcing the ink to abandon the poster- board surface, the red and black migrating down its face like refugees through a prehistoric swamp. His clean— shaven grin spreads across his squinched, ovoid face, ten wrinkles below the wisps of thin, milk- white hair that drift from under his cap. He reminds Liz and Wester of their grandfathers, though neither of them voice this recollection.

"Hello," he smiles, genially, removing some of the ominousness from their surroundings.

"Hi," says Liz over the sound of the defroster. "We were wondering if you could help us— "

"Lost, eh?" smiles the old man. "It's easy to gets lost in this part of the world, yeah? Well where you tryin' to get to, kids?"

Liz smiles at Wester, in spite of herself. "Hon?"

"Oh, yeah," Wester replies, leaning over the emergency break towards the old man. "We're looking for the Red River Inn, near the Convention Center."

The sign- carrier removes his cap, scratches his head. "Hmm. Red River Inn, you say? I can't rightly..." He pauses, sign drooping and falling from his shoulder, clattering, forming an echo that bounces off of the concrete and steel structures and echoing down the road. His rheumy eyes roll back into his head, and his cap drops from his hand onto the sidewalk below, drifting back and forth in the breeze unnaturally, like a red knit feather, or an oak leaf in autumn. The man clutches his chest under his coat, moans, and collapses, crumples into a heap.

Wester throws open his door, tries to get out but his seatbelt holds him in until he fumbles down to his lap and unbuckles it. He dashes around the front of the car to the man, where Liz already crouches over the old man's form, her hand on his wrist. "What the hell?" he asks.

"Looks like a heart attack," says Liz, "but his heart's still beating. It's beating like crazy, though," and it thumps, almost audibly, as if he'd just climbed a steep incline that had turned his heart into a bongo. "Just our luck."

"We've got to help him," says Wester. He leans down over the form, kicks the sign out of the way. "Mister? Mister, can you hear me?" A soft moan crawls out from between the man's pallid lips, and Wester begins to rifle through the pockets of his white suit and overcoat.

"What are you doing?" asks Liz.

"Maybe he has some medication or something, or at least some ID." He extracts a Gideon's Bible, three black marbles, and a half- eaten chocolate bar, a crusty business card from a Denny's restaurant, but no wallet, no medicine, nothing useful. He stands, sighs. "We've got to get him to a hospital."

Liz rises, scowling. "Damn it, Wester, where? What the hell can we do here? You have 'the most important meeting of your life' in a few hours, remember?"

"We can't just leave him here," Wester replies, curtly. He opens the car's back door and begins tossing the ingredients of the bench seat into the trunk.

Liz holds her head in her hands, would cradle herself if she could. "Why not?" she finally says. Wester simply looks at her.

"We didn't even have a full conversation with him," she continues. "He's obviously homeless, probably drunk, and he's carrying a sign around in the middle of the emptiest city I've ever been in. I say we try to make him as comfortable as possible, we can leave him with a blanket, and somebody's sure to come by in a couple of hours."

"And see what?" asks Wester, loudly. "Another guy asleep on the side of the road? He could be dead by the time somebody finds him. We've got to get him to a hospital, Liz. Help me load him into the back." He places the washed— out sign into the trunk.

Liz trembles. "Fine. Fine. It's your meeting, after all. But you're driving this time."

Wester doesn't mind; the adrenaline coursing out of his kidneys makes him feel like he could give a lion a shave. "Fine. I'll drive."

They heft the unconscious figure, surprisingly heavy, into the back seat. Liz finds a blanket in the trunk, off- handedly tosses it over him, and sulks into the passenger side, grabs her sweater and dons it hastily. Wester takes a moment to secure the old man, tucks the blanket into the crevasse between the horizontal and the vertical, and hops behind the wheel. "I think I saw a hospital somewhere near here on that map. Can you check for me?" He turns the key while Liz, embittered and exhausted, reaches to the floor and unravels the map, shaking it pointedly.

"If this antediluvian map can be trusted," she says, "there's a hospital about twenty blocks to the south of here. 'Our Lady of Sorrows'- what a great name for a hospital. Turn left here. Hopefully we can get there before I die of sleep deprivation."

"Nobody told you to stay awake the whole ride," he retorts, jerking the car into motion. "You had a good seven hours to sleep while I drove. And drove. And drove. Through the rain and the heaviest traffic."

"I can't sleep in cars," she recites, as she has so many times before. "I can only sleep in large, soft beds, with sheets and pillows and not sitting straight up. And you could have asked me to drive, but you didn't say anything, so I didn't worry about it. Now turn right."

"Whatever," Wester sighs. "Anyway, if it makes you happier, we'll just drop him off, make sure he's looked after, and head out. Somebody at the hospital should be able to give us directions, at least to a gas station."

"Fine. Like I said, I'm not the one who'll be missing some important meeting. Now just keep going straight, and it should eventually be on the right."

Despite the slight and timid evidence of morning to the east, markedly subdued behind a low sheet of clouds, the city remains vacuous, and they pass only a few cars, mostly yellow, city-owned maintenance trucks. As they near their destination, the air directly in front of the headlights begins to solidify, takes form as a chorus of cloudy strings, as the clouds demote themselves to a thick fog, travelling down to the ground, the walls of moisture, which had been touching the stratosphere, now casting the entire city into a tepid stew of formless shapes and dishonest lanterns. Wester decelerates to just above a creep in the dangerous viscosity, the car's lights hovering just a few meters in front of the car. The stillness of the fog is broken only by the solidity of the silence in the car.

"There," says Liz, pointing out a suddenly appearing sign which reads, in Gothic letters, "Our Lady of Sorrows Hospital."

Wester pulls into a small parking lot, scans for a door which the fog must be obscuring. "I can't see a way in. Looks like a poor excuse for a hospital, that's for sure."

They chuck off their seatbelts. Liz, taciturn, hops out into the fog, walks towards the nearest black and brown mass, calls out behind her "I'll see if I can find someone." Her voice hangs deeply in the mist, stuck for a moment while her body disappears towards the building, and Wester, slightly disconcerted, hoping that it is, indeed, a building, lights a cigarette and opens the back door.

"What was on that sign, old man?" he asks the still mass, receiving no reply. He removes the blanket, places it in the trunk over the back seat, and checks the man's pulse, finding, to his relief, the heart still beating. He notices for the first time a slight smell of almonds wafting from the man, or perhaps vanilla, and it disassociates him for a moment, the fog becoming a mist of scent, carrying him to his boyhood home and his mother's penchant for lighting dozens of vanilla candles at important meals. He can't remember how his mother's holiday dinners tasted; he can only remember a symphony of ham and turkey and chicken and mashed potatoes with a vanilla overture.

"You will please put out that cigarette, young man," intones a sturdy voice, female, but not Liz's, from the direction of the building. "If this person did indeed have a cardiac arrest," it continues, followed by a stocky nun, rather archetypal, in full black habit and scowl, "the last thing he needs is your second- hand smoke." Wester stubs out the smoke on his shoe, places the butt in his pocket for later.

Liz follows behind the Sister, as do two orderlies with a gurney which lulls noiselessly through the fog, onto which they are eventually able to foist the man, complete with sign. "It's just a tiny place, more like a clinic," says Liz, "run by an order of nuns. This is Sister Maria, and she's the only one who can talk right now. The rest of them have taken a vow of silence."

"You'll please follow me," shouts Sister Maria, breaking the fog with her voice.

"Look," starts Wester, "I have a really important meeting to get to in a couple of hours, and we just need to— "

But the nun, complete with entourage, has already been swallowed by the fog. Wester exhales. "Maybe they have coffee inside," he says, not expecting a reply.

"And we need to get directions, still," answers Liz, venturing around the car and touching his shoulder, lightly.

"Wester, I'm really tired, and... and I just wanted you to know that I'm so exhausted that I'm not thinking clearly. Back there, when that guy collapsed... well, I didn't really think we should just leave him there."

"I know," smiles Wester, putting his arm around her. "You're not really like that. That's why I still hang out with you. Sometimes." He grins. "We're both ridiculously worn out. We need sleep, and we need it fast. Let's go play twenty questions with some nuns and find this God- damned hotel." She circles his waist with her arm and tiredly leads him up the wooden stairs to the door.

The hospital looks more like what a wandering dervish from Thirteenth Century Crimea would expect than the large, white and sterile interior Wester had anticipated. Comfortable velvet- lined benches queue around a small waiting room, decorated in oak and teakwood, carved with meticulous Medieval representations of

Christ and the apostles healing the sick and wounded and ill- at-
ease, as if iconography had entered the world of three- dimensional
technology. On the screen of a short, primitive, black- and- white
television, the only visible reminder of the Modern Era, news
anchors, seeming laconically to emulate the prioress's vows, jabber
without words, the volume turned down. Black iron sconces emit
the soft lighting, flickering through the crannies and caverns of the
wooden reliefs and transmitting small photonic messages to the
ocean of fog visible outside the round windows.

For a moment, thinking of how interesting it would be to
see a manta ray lope or drift through the fog, Wester wonders if he
and Liz haven't boarded some sinister, nun- filled submarine from
the Middle Ages, a relic of an underwater Crusade that failed. Sister
Maria, thick and blackly decorated, scrawls onto the top layer of a
ream of paper at a dull gray- brown reception desk, motions to the
couple to approach. The bowels of the building must have absorbed
the orderlies and the old man— only the anchoritic physicians
occasionally glide through, removing the noise from what, in any
other hospital, would be the busiest section of all.

Wester and Liz take a seat at the low bench across from
Sister Maria, the perspective offered by their position forcing the
nun to loom over her desk when she speaks. "It was indeed a
cardiac arrest, but everything's under control now. What is your
relation to the patient?"

"None, actually," answers Wester. "We stopped to ask him
for directions, and he just collapsed."

"I see," Maria breathes, jotting on a form but not looking at
them. "And this older fellow, where did you find him?"

"Down by those warehouses. By the train- yard?"

"Where were you going?" Sister Maria scratches her left eye.

Liz places her hand on Wester's knee. "We were— still are, actually— trying to find the Convention Center. Wester has a meeting— "

"Hm. And you stopped for what reason?"

"To ask him for directions."

Another nun, young and less authoritative, emerges from a swinging door behind Sister Maria and leans over to scribble something on a notepad. Maria glances at the note, exclaims "I see. You're correct." She dismisses the girl, crumples the note and places it in a desk drawer, hidden from view of the couple. "Now then, this gentleman was carrying something, was he not?"

"Yes, he was carrying a sign," replies Liz, crossing her legs and smoothing her skirt.

"And what did it say?" Maria asks the questions matter- of-factly, like a holy bureaucrat, seemingly less concerned about the patient than about the facts which surround him, the construct of sensory objects taken in by eye and ear that make up the bulk of one's impressions.

Wester, slightly put off by her businesslike comportment but anxious to be on his way, tries to steal a look at the form, estimate how many further questions there would be before they were released. "I'm not sure," he says, unable to read through the Sister's beefy hands. "The rain had washed away the ink, so we couldn't be certain."

Sister Maria exhales, sounding far more exasperated than the situation merits. She turns to Liz. "What about you? Did you see what the sign said?"

Liz looks aside to Wester, confused. "No, like he said, we couldn't tell. It was dark and foggy, and the ink ran."

"Dark and foggy, eh?" clucks the Sister. "I thought you found him by the train- yards. If so, it wouldn't have been foggy when you found him. The fog wouldn't have developed until you were at least part of the way here." She begins scratching at the ream of paper once more.

Wester grumbles. "What difference does that make? We don't know the guy, never seen him before this morning, stopped to ask for directions. He groans, clutches his chest, topples over, drops his sign, and we bring him here. That's it, the whole story, the entire thing. And now we just want to ask you for some directions and get out of here." He stands. "Look, I need to use a restroom. Can you point me to it?" Liz smiles, tries to take the edge off of Wester's abruptness. "We've been on the road for twelve hours. We're both very tired."

Sister Maria smiles, or rather moves the corners of her mouth in an attempt to make a smile, points with the pen to a hall opening covered in meringue- colored curtains, which, had they been slightly less tired, they would have noticed sooner. "Restroom. Down the hall, up the stairs to the left. Please stay on the beaten path, as our staff is very busy today and doesn't need any distraction."

"I'll be back in a minute," mutters Wester, squeezing Liz's hand, and he parts the curtains as if removing gauze from a corpse. Liz smiles, turns back to Maria. Wester hears the women continue playing question- and- answer until the curtain closes, and the lack of tonality in the hall surprises him. Six blank doors break the continuity of cream- colored walls with their solid, cherry wainscoting, and as Wester strides slowly towards his destination, he wonders again whether he'll make it to his meeting. He has to make it to his meeting. "Busy," he grouses. "About as busy as a slow day on a slug farm."

He mounts the stairs to the bathroom and stands at the

antiseptic porcelain urinal, feeling the thin layer of stubble on his chin as he relieves himself for the first time in four hours. No wonder the nun treated them with such disdain, he thinks— they must look atrocious. His chin feels as though it's been sowed with crops of hair by tiny rabbits, and he desperately wishes he'd thought to bring his razor from the car. He stops long enough at the sink to wash his face in cold, metallic- tasting water, unable to tell if the dirty fluorescent light accounts for his skin's lack of tone and texture, or if his pastiness comes from stress, a long drive, the patent and inescapable frustration of nearing the end of a journey but not being able to complete it.

Stepping back into the hall, Wester decides not to worry about it too much. It wouldn't be long now, just a quick jaunt back downstairs, a few questions from the only talking nun in the place, and they'd be on their way to the comfort of the deep, hotel- style beds and industrial- strength hotel- style heaters in the Red River Inn. Of course, he'd only have time for a quick nap himself before he had to be off to the meeting, but he didn't get paid to sleep. After a few steps, he takes a quick look at his surroundings, the hall, wonders for a moment how he managed to turn himself around. Weren't there twelve doors the last time? Now there are eight, and he leans against an itinerant coat- rack to get his bearings. There are the stairs. . . .

He decides he must have taken the wrong staircase, and moves to climb back to the restroom when he notices an opening beyond one of the doors that, if his inner compass is any good, leads back in the direction of the waiting room. As it has been for the last few hours, awakeness surges through him in random increments, his third or fourth wind arriving, replacing his second or third. With a skip and a hop, he turns into the opening only to find himself staring at a wall, blank except for an antique black and white photo, framed by an intricately gilded nouveau metalwork depicting olives on the vine, mottled orbs and leaves of more bronze than gold, which end in wax- encased candelabra, dusty and unused. The photo, sepia and sun- faded, seems to depict fruit pickers in an orchard, the image too faded to denote just what they had been picking. Nonetheless, Wester stands for a moment, fascinated by the rugged, smiling faces of a family of, he assumes, migrant workers, holding old- fashioned wooden bushels, like the bottom of ale- casks cut loose and filled with fruit. The man, who seems to be the father, crouches in front of a tree with wide, serrated leaves, balances a large basket on his head with one hand and, with the other, clutches the hand of a small brown- haired girl in a frilly white dress. The girl can't be more than three or four, and she proffers an indeterminate ovoid shape to the photographer, clutching it tightly, like a toy, in a way that makes Wester wonder whether she'd actually hand over the fruit if asked.

Every now and again, it's possible to become lost in an image, in an idea or a combination of sensations that erupts a nostalgia because the sensations are arranged just so, and the perception floats for a moment, disembodied, disproving the innate subjectivity of the universe. Wester knows, realizes, then and there, that these fruit pickers didn't depend on him at all for their survival. They never knew him, would never know him, were not created by his thoughts. These people existed, just like he exists, just like Liz and the old man and the nuns and Sister Maria exist outside of the flighty and fanciful realm created by humans in their quest for evolutionary satisfaction. The smell, the absence of sound, the echoing vision of the fruit pickers, the little girl, most likely long dead by now, or very, very old, danced through the hall and around the doors of the hospital into an absolute, an objectivity inaccessible to most everyday thoughts, but, like six colorful keys that unlock a genie's treasure chamber only when turned consecutively, they bring Wester out of a miasma by taking him into one, broken only by a strange whining at his feet.

When he looks down, away from the photo, he wonders

why he hadn't noticed the dog before, when he came into the alcove. He chalks it up to exhaustion. The dog, a smooth, medium-sized cattle dog of some kind, whines again, gazing into Wester's eyes with a gentle intelligence, alternating eyebrow raises. Its wide, black eyes and large, pointed, ten- and- two ears and hyena-spotted skin give its face an appearance not unlike a cross between a fruit bat and a snub— nosed bat. After it whines again unthreateningly, Wester kneels and pats the dog on its wide head, and it places its left paw on his knee, scratching lightly down twice. It bows its head, but carries Wester's petting hand in the sweep of the bow firmly with its forehead, never giving. The dog, just looking at Wester, blinks, and Wester, just looking at the dog, blinks. Wester shakes his head as the dog trots away down the hall, and, thinking to himself that he had no other real option, follows, turns right, and passes through the curtains, which separate the hall from the waiting room, and the curtains glow with the light of the sun. He parts the curtains, shields his eyes because the light streams in intensity through the porthole— like windows. When his eyes adjust to the brightness of the sun, he notices that neither Liz or Sister Maria are at the desk. Instead, a young, pretty nun sits in front of the ream of paper, jotting random words onto random lines. "Excuse me?" he asks her.

She looks up at him, smiles politely, "Can I help you, sir?"

"Yes, I was here earlier with Sister Maria and a girl? About an old man?"

"Ah yes, we were all wondering about you. Sister Maria's shift ended. She's back in Service now, renewing her vow of silence."

"And the girl?"

"Yes, she's there on the bench by the door. Asleep, I should think." Like Maria before her, she points with the pen in the direction of Liz, who indeed sleeps on one of the benches.

He thanks the nun, and walks to Liz, bends over her and whispers. "Honey? Wake up."

She slowly opens her eyes, grumbling. "Where the hell have you been?"

He notices two things: first, that the television volume has been turned up, and the newscasters were talking, loudly, with pseudo— classical music playing in the background, and secondly, that he couldn't find the dog. "Where did that dog go?" he asks the nun at the desk.

"What dog?" she replies.

"Your dog, doesn't it live here? It seemed to know where it was going."

"We don't have a dog here, I can assure you."

The volume on the television set increases, and short, bursting staccatos fill it. Shit, thinks Wester, I missed my meeting.

3. Excerpt From a Letter to the Colonies

...Snant, our leader, essentially in media res, 'in the middle of things,' sat at the head of the devilishly wooden table, toying with his feathered brown fedora as if it contained a kitten. "It's unusual," he mumbled, scanning the yellowed paper one last time like a sheet of banana, "but I like it." You know Snant, Emma, and how he always manages to say what nobody expects, but everyone knows he'll say.

"Multi- hued but not complex?" asked Roland.

"Reminds me of a picture frame I saw once. I don't recall the painting that was in it. It's like that: a frame that's more memorable than the painting it surrounds. Oz, Camille, you guys in on this?" Snant asked, putting his hat on and standing, thumbs through his suspenders.

Oz and Camille, in the corner, nodded their heads in unison, and Oz leaned over to kiss her on the cheek.

"Good. Alons, how about you?"

I nodded as well. No "I'm in" today, no "Sign me up!" The implications of the job danced subtly by each of us, a thought process you're no doubt familiar with by now, and each of us knew that there was no "in," or "out," or anything other than a nod or the absent silence that signified unanimity. The silence being a non-issue, we picked up the gear and hopped into the van.

Oz, long blonde hair tied into a ponytail, grabbed the all-important satchel, a navy- blue duffel bag from the National Library, that Snant promptly snatched seconds later. "Uh- uh," he growled. "I think I'd better hold onto this."

"What, you don't think I can handle it?" asked Oz. "Shit, I did five jobs for McGandry back in Sydney, and he's the one that referred me to you. You can't say that ain't a fine record to have."

"Oh no worries, my friend. I trust you implicitly. It's simply that I want my...energy...around this bag. Get it?" Snant was like that: there really wasn't anything in the bag just yet, but he needed his aura, his presence, he claimed, to coexist with the container of whatever he happened to be stealing that day. So he held the bag one hundred percent of the time, every time, reading it and letting it read him.

I already told you about how smoothly we pulled the act itself, and you're familiar with our tactics, so now in this letter is when I say 'cut to the chase,' and I start to talk about after the fact, when we were all in the same van but three hours later, cursing at speeds of up to three hundred kilometers an hour in a '89 Swerton as City Police whizzers buzzed overhead and we hit the Interbay tunnel at seventy. "Shit," screamed Camille, "Gotta get past 'em!"

I don't know if they have whizzers yet where you are; they're a relatively recent development. The CPD started using them last month; they're essentially modified, two- person helicopters, faster than hell, designed to hold a cop and his prisoner, and if they fall, they don't crash— the blades rotate the craft gently to the ground. The Avignon Cell blew a dozen old style copters out of the sky last year, choosing the more violent tactics that our cell abhors, even if we're all working towards the same end, so the CPD's International team came up with a lighter, faster, and safer version of the same thing. Besides, you know how bad City traffic's gotten— cops can't rightly chase anyone in cars anymore. No doubt you'll all have to worry about them soon, too. Picture giant, upright, vibrating praying mantises with rotors, and you've got the idea.

Snant, in the passenger seat, guiding Roland's arms as he tried to steer around the thickness of three o'clock rush hour, shouted, "No need to start panicking. I got us a hook- up."

"Camille, honey," Oz said, probably thinking of his damned mother, home in Toowoomba, because (like the rest of us) he was so frightened. "We got it! We got the fucking steal, didn't we? We're doing something grand, we are."

"Yeah, but the CPD!"

"The CPD's on our ass, folks," lisped Roland, spitting his beard out of his mouth with every fifth word. "For example, we're about to come out of the tunnel, and those fucking whizzers are gonna see us, no problem. Why this fucking huge van, Snant? It's like driving around Congo in a car made of ivory. You're fucking dead if they catch you, and they're sure as shit gonna catch you!"

"Van Snant, I like that," answered our unofficial headman and organizer. "From now on, call me 'Grigori van Snant.' It's my new name "

"Yeah, fuckin' great. Now Grigori, what about the fucking choppers?"

"Shit, man. You zapped the plan together, sure, but don't you think old man van Snant might have a way to outwit a few police whizzer units? Hell, brotha, you can't fight for no cause from jail, knowwhutImean? It happens I got a tunnel worker that owes me a favor. Pull over after this next curve."

Roland eased the van down from rapidity to solidity and pulled over to the side. Snant hopped out, walked around the back of the van, and Camille peeked out of the back window like a guppy through a porthole. Snant was gesturing wildly at a short, withered, elderly gentleman with a gray handlebar moustache in white and yellow overalls. The man unzipped his overalls halfway and, reaching in, removed a shining golden trumpet with a bright red mute in the bell. Removing the mute, the old man unscrewed its top and shook a key into his hand. Snant took the key, walked to the wall, which we realized was actually a door, and unlocked a huge, bronze lock.

He had to lift the door manually, and I hopped out and gave a hand. The door was rather ingeniously hidden by layers of fluorescent lichen, which stained my fingers green, and I asked Snant what got worked on behind it, what we could expect. "This is an old City Police tunnel," he said, and I let go of the door for a minute and groaned. "Shit man, don't groan like that," continued Snant. "This shit hasn't been used for decades, man, and Old Joe there, he owes me one, so we gonna get out through this thing. You think the CPD's gonna look for us right in their own damned tunnel? Forget about it. But don't mention it to the others; I don't want them to worry about it."

We hopped back in the machine and Roland guided it into the tunnel. "I still think this is fucked," he lisped, spraying. "Where does this tunnel let out?"

"Yeah," said Oz, "but imagine the looks on those cops' faces when we don't pop out of the tunnel like they expect. Pretty brilliant, I think, and I think we'll get away with this one."

"We'll be at the rendezvous point long before they ever

remember there's an old service tunnel down here," said Snant. "Don't worry your heads. Just get out the gats and nitrogen tank. We'll need 'em in about ten minutes."

The van oozed into the darkness, headlights on, as Old Joe closed the vast door behind us with an echoing but muted boom, amplified by our sense of impending doom. Camille pulled out our "weapons of mass disgustion," as Snant liked to call them, simple high- powered paint guns loaded with animal waste. There's a difference between getting hit in the face by a concentrated ball of fecal matter and getting hit hard in the face with a concentrated ball of fecal matter, and he'd correctly guessed that the weapons would cause enough confusion and horror to allow us to pull the heist. Oz reached down for the nitrogen, and Snant clutched the blue duffel bag to his chest, the one that contained the statue's green, plastic eyes. Emma, you have an Art History degree— when did people start thinking it was okay to make statues out of plastic?

After a few minutes of slurring slug- like through thick, solid darkness, a grey, adobe wall materialized in front of the van, and Roland screamed "What the fuck, Snant?!" as he pulled the van into a stop and threw open his door. The headlights illuminated the shiny, black pseudo- Cyrillic lettering that dressed the wall: CITY POLICE DEPARTMENT: ACCESS TUNNEL 12- B, RESTRICTED AREA.

Isn't it odd how Old Soviet- era deco is in vogue with the fuckin' cops? I mean, I couldn't have written it better if I'd tried.

So anyhow, we all follow Roland's lead while Snant explains to the rest that this is an old tunnel, etc., and if we just follow his lead, the CPD'll have no idea we were even in here until they find the abandoned van whenever. Oz guessed aloud that we should get a move on, as the whizzers had no doubt landed by now and stormtroopers might be in hot pursuit. I couldn't help but picture them behind us, breaking the darkness in the tunnel with clotted footsteps and lumberjack action hops across invisible logs. We'd have heard them by now, though. It's kind of curious, actually, that they didn't come right after us, and I can only guess that Old Joe had something to do with it.

The only light source, after we powered down the van, came from a dull green emanation generated by Snant's goggles. We hopped after him, as he infraredded his way through a side passage until he reached an impasse and scanned the wall with his goggles. Snant, in the spirit of things, had attached googly- eyes onto the goggles, and now he looked like a giant, shady marionette, reading the wall as if it were an incredibly absorbing novel about mathematical equations. "Ah ha," he said, and brushed away what turned out to be a net, covered in wall slime, indistinguishable from the remainder of the tunnel system, revealing the metal rungs of a ladder.

"Great," whispered Roland, reaching to be the first up, and his hand immediately flew away when Snant's arm careened to meet it.

"Don't touch yet, Roland," said the goggled one, "because your hand will be reduced to a charred mass of flesh by these hot metal rungs and you will never again be able to operate a motor vehicle with the skill you're famous for."

Roland stepped back, rubbed his wrist protectively.

Snant motioned to Oz, who pumped the liquid nitrogen out of the canister onto the ladder, a great cloud of dry ice, smelled like every damned rock concert I've ever been to. "This may not work perfectly, so everybody needs to stand back and shield their eyes."

The metal rungs of the ladder popped and bloated as the intense cold met the intense heat, generated who- knows- how, and though we couldn't make out exactly what happened until the fog lifted, we could hear the creaking and masquerading of the metal, like the sound a ghost makes in your attic when you're home by yourself and nobody else can hear it. Oz stopped spraying after a few seconds, and the rungs remained intact, made of what must've been an almost indestructible metal.

"Okay," said Snant, removing the goggles, "we only have a few minutes before the rungs start to heat up again, so everybody move it."

We piled up the ladder and through a trapdoor into a world of fur and buzzing. Snant went last, closing the trapdoor behind him, and we could now see the powerful heater attached to the metal rungs by wires, but, even stranger, hundreds of cats flowed through the room and upstairs to our left, down stairs to our right, like a Biblical Flood, but of cats. We'd come out in a room below one of the Organization's Safe Houses, and I could tell because of all of the cats, part of another 'action' you may have heard about.

"If any cops come after us," joked Oz, "they'll be the red-handed ones, not us."

Snant led us through the ankle deep herds of feline livestock. (And what do you call a multiplicity of cats, anyhow? A gaggle of cats? A pride? A mob of cats? What do you think?) "Cops won't come after us," he said. "We got that taken care of."

After heading through a veritable labyrinth filled with felines and smelling of meat, navigating our way through air conditioning units, elevator equipment, and supply closets, we finally entered a rather comfortable, if a bit shabby, standard slummy apartment, and had a chance to catch our breaths. "Where's the cat tender?" I asked, plopping down for a minute or so on a soft, hair- covered couch.

"He ain't here right now," replied Snant. "We can't afford to connect him with us; he's too busy with the other plan." Oz and Camille disappeared into another room, no doubt thinking of their own ways to relax for a minute or fifteen. Snant hopped the duffel bag onto the masonite table and extracted one of the eyes that we'd worked so hard to nab. "Beautiful, if bad art," he exclaimed, rubbing the sphere almost as if he tried to wipe away the gleam. "Our man in Burma is gonna be pleased as a tiny baby when he lays his eyes on these eyes, baby. Ain't no way they watchin' us from downtown, not quite yet. Hey, you know where Roland went off to?"

"Nope. Maybe he had to take a piss. I haven't seen him since the cat room."

"Shit, I'm hungry. I'm going to see what's in the kitchen. You want anything?"

"Nah, I'm gonna close my eyes for a few minutes. Why don't you close those eyes we stole, Snant? Don't want your prints all over 'em."

"Good point." He wiped the eyes off with his basketball jersey, put them back in the duffel bag, and smirked into the kitchen, tall the whole while.

I guess I must've dozed off for a few minutes, thinking of you, sweetest, because the next thing I knew, three giant, black emperor beetles crashed and slammed through the flimsy, pressboard door, and it took a second for me to realize that they weren't beetles, they were cops. Somebody'd ratted us out.

"FREEZE, CITY POLICE!" shouted the cops, and then I got to see why Snant's reputation as a categorical bad-ass is huger than the man himself. From the kitchen, he tosses three handfuls of what I later learned was fish guts, which it certainly smelled like, all over the chitinous skins of the CPDers. Momentarily surprised, the cops didn't have enough time to react when he flashed out of the kitchen, long arm outstretched like a hovercrane, and tore open the door to the tunnel, releasing a cloudy stampede of half-starved cats, who flowed like a flash flood towards the ultra-shocked policemen, and Snant and I grabbed our air- guns and bolted for the front door.

"Someone sold us out," I screamed, and we had to toss ourselves upstairs because we could already hear the drone of the whizzers outside. "Where's Roland? It was that fat, lisping motherfucker!"

Up seven flights, Snant shouted "How do we know? Could have been Oz or Camille or Old Joe. No way of saying."

"We should have taken the tunnel back," I said, checking each door, trying to find one that was unlocked.

"No way, man. If more cops come in here, they gonna head down it to find out where the cops came from, and then we'd be trapped on all ends."

"Like we're not trapped on all ends here?!" We rounded another corner and began trying the next set of doors.

"We'll figure something out, my man," he answered, as a knob turned so wonderfully in my hand and we crashed into a domestic scene.

A short, dark woman, dressed in a robe, with thick, fat lips, crouched down on the floor, cleaning up after the evening meal of her young son. When she picked up his plate and held it there, seeing us in vast chasms of surprise, I remembered that she sometimes waited tables down at the Open Whelk Café— remember the place?— and I smiled and she started screaming when she saw our guns. Snant slammed and locked the door, and creaked through the peephole, out of breath. We made it a point never to aim at someone you weren't going to shoot, so we left our guns down to put the chick at ease.

The lady picked up her child, her arms wrapped around the

fuzzy, pink bunny on the kid's pajamas, and I picked up the phone, pulled the cord from the wall. "Listen, miss, I know this must look a little something like a big budget action movie, a 'high octane thrill ride,' but we really need a favor. We can pay— "

WHACK!

She kicked a pearled, fluffed slipper in the air, and it contacted me square in the forehead, between the proverbial eyes!

"Ow, hey!"

"They're not coming yet, man," Snant said of the police. "Maybe Oz and Camille are putting up a fight. I think I just heard a shot."

I, too busy thinking 'ow, hey!' to respond, tried again. "Miss, that hurt!"

"You bastard!" she screamed, and kicked the other slipper at me. Luckily, I saw this one coming and had the sense to duck, but Snant didn't know it was on the way, and it slammed into the back of his elongated head, knocking off his hat.

He turned around, hand to head, picked up his hat and replaced it. "What did you do to her, Alons?"

"Snant, we just stormed into her house carrying guns," I reply, as she begins wailing full lunged and chanting a loud string of expletives in Spanish, which sets the kid off bleating, too, like those klaxon alarms you've been telling me about. Not a good thing when the CPD's on your ass like a goat on a mule, right?

"Miss?" asked Snant, softly, "can you please quiet down?"

The woman stopped yelling in Spanish, and started up on me in English. On me, personally! That, my sweet, cannot be described, how you burst into some chick's room to get away from the CPD and then she starts laying into you for one of the craziest reasons you've ever heard: seems last week I'd forgotten to tip her.

"You son of a bitch," she shouts, "I've had it with you shitty customers and you can't possibly understand, you fucking moron, that I have a god- damned daughter to fucking feed and you didn't tip," etc., etc., etc., like a Scientologist trying to advance to the next level or whatever, and I couldn't, for the life of me, remember having not tipped. I always tip.

"I always tip," I started, and she pulled out a cellular phone.

"I always call the cops," she says, flipping open the phone, her fingers starting to dial.

"For the love of god, no!" shouted Snant, and tried to fit as much information he could into the smallest possible number of words: "Miss, I know he tips. I've seen him tip with my very two eyes. Please don't call the cops. Look, you don't call the cops, we'll owe you whatever. Whatever you want, you got. Cash? Cars? We have some very powerful friends, miss, and we can set you up."

Under her mop of curly hair, she looked up for a second and stopped dialing. "Whatever I want?" she finally asked.

"Most anything you want," agreed Snant, hoping she didn't ask for the millions of dollars that we could never give her.

"I'll be back here in a minute," she said, closing the phone and taking the child into the kitchen.

Snant and I glanced at one another. "Why the fuck didn't you tip her, muthafucka?"

"I did tip her," I exclaim. "I always tip. You said you saw me tip her!"

"I didn't see shit, man. We better be damned sure to get her what she wants."

From the kitchen, her voice traveled to our ears. "Eight dollars and three cents." She entered the room again, calculator in hand.

"What?" Snant and I asked simultaneously.

"Eight dollars and three cents," she said, pointing at me, "is twenty percent of your forty dollar and fifteen cent meal. A Reuben, a water, and a seaweed salad. That comes to forty dollars and fifteen cents, and as a good tip is twenty percent, I want you to tip me, and tip me good. So it's gonna cost eight dollars and three cents to keep me from turning both your asses right in."

Snant sighs. "Whatever, lady." He pulls a tenner out of his wallet and steps for her, but she holds up her hand to stop him.

"Nope. He has to pay it," she says, pointing a curled, blue fingernail at my forehead.

"This is ridiculous," says Snant.

"Hey, that's cool. I'll just get the money from the CPD," she threatened, lifting the phone. Didn't make sense, of course, but we got the gist of her message.

Sighing, I stepped forward and whispered into Snant's ear, "Hey, can you do me a favor and loan me ten bucks? I'll getcha back tomorrow."

"No way, man. I need this for the cab ride home later, provided we make it."

"Come on, I don't have any cash on me right now. You know I'm good for it."

"Just like you always tip, right?" Half of Snant's face curled in disdain. "Shee- it," he exclaimed, and tossed the tenner at me.

"Thanks, man." I handed it over to the waitress, and she reached into the pocket of her robe, pulled something out that she opened up in her hand to me.

"One ninety- seven is your change." A crumpled bill and a few coins. I took 'em. I swear I tipped that woman, Emma. You know I always tip. "Now you get out of my house. I ain't gonna call the cops, but this ain't no hangout for criminals, neither."

I know, criminals every time, huh?

But it didn't matter. Actually, the whole scene evaporated, disappeared, shoved itself away in uselessness. Shit, I thought, it was no concern of the cops whether I tipped her or didn't tip her or paid her at all or never even saw her, and the cops opinion mattered to me almost immediately, when they busted down the door and arrested me and Snant and hauled us away to a wagon.

Oz and Camille were there, too, battered but amazingly not completely dead. All the CPDers who'd been covered in filth from their earlier scuffle with our two comrades left us with a couple of clean ones, who started hovering and called us into their headquarters.

"That shit Roland ratted us out," scowled Oz. "And we're done for, mates."

Camille gripped him.

They described their shoot— out. Apparently they'd heard the cat stampede and knew something'd happened that should concern them, so they grabbed their gats and hit the living room just as the second cop freed the first from the feline. The two policemen stood like altered turtles, and upon seeing Oz and Camille, immediately regretted it, because Oz and Camille doused them with the waste pellets. Bullets of shit hit them at about sixty miles per hour, got them confused for enough time for Camille to pull the Aussie around the corner into the bathroom. Suddenly more cops were at the bathroom door, and our two friends held out in the bathtub for as long as they could. Suddenly one of the stormtroopers pulled his weapon and fired into the ceiling, the shot that Snant had caught, and Oz and Camille knew they'd had it, so they gave in. None of us really wants to get shot, right?

Anyhow, gotta wrap this up.

About fifteen minutes into the drive, Oz noticed that we weren't heading for CPD headquarters at all. We were being taken somewhere else, out of the city, to a ranch— style house in the country, on a sympathizer farm in a secret location, that was run by guess who? Us! Turns out the wagon drivers were a couple of our guys, and the fuckers waited to tell us until we'd landed because they thought it'd be funny. Bastards.

We were led into the debriefing room, and Snant whispered "you better give me back my ten after all this shit, Alons."

You know what a standard DR room looks like. The four of us sat around the table, too shocked and happy to be angry or worried, the trepidation dissolving like fleece from a shorn sheep, and when the Director walked in with Roland, we couldn't fucking believe it!

Oz was up and heavy. "You turned us in, you fuck!" he shouted, lurching for the bearded lisper.

"Hold it, Oz," said the Director. "This operation was a complete success. The statue was demolished completely once you nabbed the eyes."

"Complete success?!" yelled Camille. "We almost got shot by the fucking CPD!"

"Statue was destroyed?" asked Snant. "I don't remember hearing that the statue'd be blown up."

"We know," lisped the unpopular van driver. "You've made a lovely distraction."

The Director sat and began again. "You five were picked because you're each the best at what you do." (I blushed, hon.) "And we needed the best to evade the cops once Roland called them in and keyed them in on your location. They thought they were only going after the thieves, which gave us a chance to get the real work done."

So you can see what I mean, Ella, about how you can never be sure what's what in this Organization. We were a red herring. They needed us to hold off the cops for as long as possible so the demolition men could get in. But I must say, and this is basically what I was writing to tell you about, that I wasn't as set off by the Director's exposition as by what happened next, which is the thing I mentioned earlier.

Roland turned and looked at me. I mean, he really glared at me, like for some reason I'd personally asked him how many times he'd dreamed of killing his own mother, that's how strong he glared at me. "Alons," he said, spraying the table with lisp. "Alons, just so you know, last week, at the Open Whelk Café, I stole your tip from the table. But now I can give you this." He handed me eight dollar bills and tossed three pennies on the Formica surface of the table in front of me, and they whirred and whirred before stopping flat.

Ella, tell your people—

[Letter Ends Here]

4. The Milk Truck Incident

On the way to the barber shop, Howe purchased a box of leftover Valentine's Day candy for twenty- five cents from the corner market, and found that every single heart- shaped pellet of candy in his box was autographed with, instead of the banal and romantic expressions cribbed from dime- store romance novels, the name 'BRIAN,' in large, red, capital letters. Needless to say, Howe, fascinated by this bewildering turn of confectionary events, decided that eating the candy would put an unfortunate end to an inexplicable phenomenon, and he supposed he'd better hang onto them for a while.

("Why didn't you eat them?" Paula later inquired of him. "I don't think that it's 'needless to say.'"

"I dunno," Howe answered. "I guess the wrongness of it all kept me from popping one into my mouth. It's similar to ... imagine getting a Fortune Cookie and finding that the fortune inside had the word 'PIANO' on it. Just 'PIANO,' nothing else. Would you eat the cookie?"

"It'd be too late," she answered.)

After discovering the anomalous candies, Howe stuffed the

open box into his pocket and ran his left hand through his hair. It had been too long since he'd had a haircut; his coiffure jaunted merrily off of his head at odd angles. It wasn't actually too long, but it had been at least a month since he'd had even a trim, and the eruption of hair annoyed him. Today that would change, until another month had passed and his hair again began to encroach upon the three inches of personal space that surrounded his head.

("How would it be too late?" he eventually asked Paula.

"Because," she answered, "you eat the cookie first and then read the fortune, or else it won't come true. I never read my fortune until I've sucked the cookie crumbs out from between my teeth and run my tongue around the inside of my mouth to guarantee that there's no cookie left. So by the time I saw 'PIANO,' I'd have already eaten the entire cookie."

"That's crazy talk," said Howe. "I've never heard that before. Where'd you get the idea that you have to finish the entire cookie?"

"I can't recall. I guess I read it somewhere. Maybe in Sand Quarterly." Over the past week, she and Howe had dreamed up Sand Quarterly as an imaginary reference for any fact they knew to be true but didn't know why. 'I read about it in Sand Quarterly' generally and firmly established the fact that you knew one hundred percent that what you had said contains the infallible truth, but you don't know why or where you'd originally heard it. The invented magazine had supplied them with every odd bit of unverifiable information, from the story of Alexander the Great's experiences with Diogenes the Cynic, to the gestation period of the northern Sea Otter. If it had been in Sand Quarterly, its veracity could not be questioned.

But, this entire conversation took place later.)

First, Howe needed to have his hair cut. He shoved the candies into his jacket pocket and continued along Main Street to

Mr. Salinas' Barber Shop. He hated having his hair cut: it meant at least twenty minutes of listening to Salinas not talk: snip, buzz, all of the sounds you don't want to hear when someone isn't talking, but the small talk is the kind of pseudo— intimate blather that only increases the apparent duration of the stay. If you get your hair cut every three weeks, thought Howe, then the Barber has just enough time to forget everything you told him on your last visit, and asks you the same questions as before, so you feel you should answer the same way; but that was three weeks ago, and you don't remember the banal and insignificant things you did three weeks ago, and you end up creating entirely false banal, insignificant events, which are not the kinds of events that people should create, but you don't want to tell your barber the true and intimate personal details of your life. By the time your next visit comes, three weeks later, you're so trapped in the cycle of creating humdrum events in order to fool the Barber into thinking you have a normal, humdrum life, that you're still covering your tracks from the last visit by creating new humdrum events to cover up the fake events you'd created the week before. By the time the end of this saga rolls around— which, if you have a regular Barber who you see every three weeks, will end in his (or your) death— you've created an entirely new and uninteresting life for yourself.

Your best bet, thought Howe, is to keep your mouth shut.

Howe entered the shop through the glass door, taking a moment to curse at a poster of the President that Salinas had taped on the front of the door. He whistled, sat in a mauve, vinyl chair near the door, and flipped through some archaic magazines that coated the top of a small table. If the visit went as he hoped it would, Salinas wouldn't be in a talkative mood. He only rarely spoke, which spurred Bertrand to visit him regularly in the first place. However, when Salinas did decide to get chatty, everything emerged— religion, politics, sex, you name it— and as Salinas had perhaps the most conservative views in town and Howe was something of a liberal... well, you can see how having a political enemy standing over you with a pair of shears and a razor would be a bit unsettling

("I can certainly see that," said Paula at a later date.)

indeed. So Howe had no recourse but to sit, silently, listening to the man orate lustily on 'glory' and 'freedom' and his patriotic love for a political system that Howe found primitive and silly.

As Howe fingered the latest edition of Modern Haircut, he eavesdropped on the beefy, mustachioed man who sat in front of Salinas, getting a trim. "There are certain kinds of dogs," he was saying, "that are bred for certain kinds of people. Take the poodle, for instance. Obviously," he belched, "poodles are made for small old women, who enjoy a dog that can be styled and pampered."

Salinas's face turned red and he clipped at a furious pace. "That isn't so, necessarily," he responded. Howe began to worry: is this large man going to get Salinas worked up? This didn't bode well for the avoidance of conversation that he so desired.

The fat man shifted, caused Salinas to stop clipping for a moment. The barber wiped his brow. "I own a poodle," he said, "and I find that Georg is no old lady's dog, I tell you!"

The man in the chair finished shifting, rested his thick arms on the armrests of the chair where they spilled over the sides, and began to sweat profusely, compelling Howe to glance at the thin heater over the door, which pumped warm but stale air into the room, the kind of atmosphere that makes you wake up thirsty if you fall asleep in it. Next to the heating system perched a small black and white television set with the volume turned all the way down. On the screen, the President waved his hands merrily as he delivered a speech of some kind before a congregate of what seemed to be kerchiefed, Old World washerwomen.

The sweating man stuttered as Salinas began clipping his hair once again with a black electric shaver. "Oh," he stuttered, raising his voice unnecessarily over the buzz of the clipper, "I ... I of course mean toy poodles. Not the standard breed, but the tiny ones, you know... I'm sure your Georg is a fine specimen, a fine dog indeed."

"I don't see what difference that makes," said Salinas. "A poodle's a poodle, be it a toy, a standard, what have you. One is just smaller than the other, not more or less intelligent. I think you just don't like poodles."

"Perhaps I should edit my words," said the man, wiping the sweat off of his handlebar moustache and grinning idiotically. He seemed to want to turn around, show Salinas by the look on his face that he spoke with utter sincerity, and Howe had to lift the magazine to cover his smile in spite of himself. "Poodles are fine. It's those damned tiny Mexican dogs. They're awful and pink, and they yap constantly. It's the barking that annoys me."

"I see," said Salinas, stolid but humourless. "So you just don't like dogs in general, is that it? Are you more of a cat man? You insult my dog while I cut your hair. Perhaps I should call the police."

("I couldn't believe it," Howe later told Paula. "Upon being called a 'cat man,' the heavyset individual turned beet- red, redder than he had been before. He looked like a tomato covered in morning dew, and had about as much to say in response."

"I like your comparisons," she answered. "They make me laugh. You're a very descriptive person. Does this mean that you write?" But this occurred in a conversation that was yet to come.)

Before the cat man could answer Salinas, the barber brushed the hair off of his shoulders and whipped the apron off of him. "You're done," said the barber.

"Salinas, my friend, you know I didn't mean anything by it. There's no need to drag the cops into this. I had forgotten that you have a standard poodle, that's all. Please accept my apologies. Hey, the worst of all dogs is better than the best cat, right?" He hopped out of the seat with both feet and a thud, and turned around, simultaneously looking at his head in the mirror and taking a wad of cash out of his front pocket. "This is a wonderful haircut, as usual, Salinas. Here's some extra for you"

"Thank you, Austin," said Salinas, shaking out the apron and taking the money. "Please, I didn't take offense. I just wanted to make sure you're a real man, a dog man, not someone who prefers the company of those damned slinky felines, if you know what I mean."

"I know what you mean," said Austin, laughing, and nervously rubbing his fleshy neck with an overripe hand. "Listen, I'll see you later. Three weeks, right?"

"Right," said Salinas, motioning to Howe. "Hello, Mr. Howe. Please have a seat. Goodbye, Austin."

"Bye, Salinas." Austin shambled out of the barber's small shop into the street, letting in a momentary blast of cold.

("So go back for a minute," said Paula. "The barber threatened to call the police if Austin liked dogs instead of cats? Was he serious? They wouldn't have come, you know; not for something as small as that."

"I think," said Howe, "that the threat was made just to scare him. Most people are frightened of the police, you know."

"I see," said Paula.)

Howe took a seat in the green vinyl barber chair and removed his glasses. The chair squeaked uncomfortably, and wheezed as Salinas pumped the chair to the appropriate level. "What'll it be today, Howe? The usual? I see you're getting shaggy, eh?"

"Just a trim," answered Howe. He could tell by Salinas' tone that the man remained irritated over the insult to his dog. When Salinas felt talkative, it always started with a snide remark about how poorly his customer treated his or her coiffure, an instantaneous judgment for which Howe couldn't blame the man; after all, hair was the man's life. He was, Howe thought to himself, a good barber— the only barber he knew of who could cut hair properly. Nonetheless, Howe thought he should introduce an innocuous topic of conversation as soon as possible, all things considered. While Salinas was turned around disinfecting his tools, Howe reached into his pocket and retrieved the mysterious box of candies, opened it and removed one of the tiny hearts. "Say," he said, "have you ever seen anything like this?"

The barber looked at the candy over his glasses. "Candy, eh? My granddaughter always brings these for me. Did you know that now they have ones that say 'Fax Me' and 'Email Me'? Not like the good old days, eh, when it was just hugs and kisses." He read the message on the front. "Now that's odd. 'Brian'? Very strange."

"The strangest part," Howe replied, "is that they all say 'Brian.' It's mysterious; I have no idea how this could possibly have happened." He passed the box to Salinas, who took it incredulously.

"This is fascinating," said the barber. "You know what I think? I think it's some kind of code, some kind of code for revolutionaries. What are the latest group calling themselves?"

"'Idealists'," Howe replied, carefully. "I think," he added.

"It's definitely a code," said the barber, handing the candies back to his customer. "Here you go. I'll bet you saved the President or somebody by accidentally intercepting these. One for the books, eh?"

("Was it a code?" asked Paula, later that week. "It does sound like something the Idealists would do. You remember the milk truck incident."

"I don't remember that," said Howe, pointedly. "I don't think it was a code. I think that maybe some bourgeois high school girl decided to make a unique gift for her boyfriend for Valentine's Day, and his name is Brian, but he never ended up receiving the candy, for some reason or another. That's one of my theories, anyhow."

"I wish you wouldn't use that term: 'bourgeois.' It has connotations, and connotations never help anyone, if you know what I mean." She smiled, brilliantly, and ran her fingers through his hair.

"Can I have a glass of water?" he asked her.)

Salinas went straight to work, trimming and buzzing away, chatting about this and that, as Howe had feared he would. At least he wasn't irritated; he guided his scissors around Howe's head as if they were a pair of trained dragonflies— the scissors flew erratically but skillfully over his split ends, and he imagined that this haircut wouldn't take too long.

About ten minutes into his cut, a dapper, suited, elderly black man, accompanied by a young blonde woman, entered the shop and sat in the waiting area. The young woman, who looked like the for five ninety- nine! That's a good deal."

The man clucked suspiciously. "That sounds too good to be true. There ain't no way you can get a whole chicken for six dollars. No way, no how. Must be a half chicken, or part of a chicken."

"No, look, says right here: 'Whole Roasted Chicken and Two

Sides from the deli: five ninety- nine. There's even a picture." She poked the picture with a sharp, bony finger.

The man took the newsprint insert and placed a pair of scratched glasses on his nose. "Well I'll be. That's some deal. A whole chicken for six dollars."

"I told you," she said. "A whole chicken for five ninety-nine."

"A whole chicken," he replied, returning the paper to the girl.

"It's some deal," she said. "Five ninety- nine!"

"A whole chicken. Mm- mm. Some deal."

"Six dollars, even."

Howe wished they would stop.

("I see what you mean about them," said Paula, when she was done. "now that you've finished telling me that part of the story. Did I scratch you?"

"Yes," replied Howe, painfully. "You did."

"It's okay," said Paula, rubbing his chest. "I didn't break the skin. So finish your story.")

As an emphatic, rolling boom accompanied by octopoid tendrils of smoke made its way down the street, causing the windows to vibrate as if they were being played by a giant violin bow, Salinas stopped clipping Howe's hair. With an oblique whine, white, streaking cracks appeared in the red lettering of the window, fracturing "SALINAS HAIRCUTTERY" into an unreadable mess. With a violent crash, the windows of the barber shop shattered, spreading glass like solid water across the floor and the sidewalk outside. The elderly man and his haggish friend stood abruptly, stopped discussing the great chicken deal; she tossed the insert aside as if she hadn't been reading it at all. Everyone but Howe rushed for the door and onto the sidewalk, a blast of cold air hitting Howe directly, as he removed the apron and followed suit, crunching glass and hair underfoot, noticing on the way that the television screen had gone blank.

("And that boom was the explosion?" asked Paula.

"I told you already. It was.")

The girl, sobbing like a depressed hyena, had tucked her face into the shoulder of the old man, who patted her arm, trying to comfort her. Salinas stood thickly by, his fists clenched as if they both held long, nail encrusted wooden clubs. "Dammit!" he said, returning to his shop with heavy and violent strides. "DAMMIT! It's like some fucking FOREIGN COUNTRY!"

About a block away, in front of 'Le Patois,' a five— star, upscale restaurant, the choking remains of what had been a city sewage truck cast a violently unquenchable odor through the neighborhood. Burning human waste and methane continued to spew licks of flame from the carcass of the truck, which rested on its haunches like a gutted boar, into the husk of the restaurant, the face of which had been demolished by the blast. The early dinner crowd poured out of the building, diners and staff alike feeling the almost unbearable stench and stepping delicately through brown puddles of raw sewage, while a business— suited manager shouted commands to two hectic chefs, who busily ignored him in favor of carrying expensive kitchen equipment out of the range of the fire. "Do you think it was a bomb?" asked the old man, with the steely but patriotic look of a veteran who still yearned for the excitement that only war or terrorism could bring.

"I'd say so," replied Howe. "I don't think trucks just blow up like that, unless they get hit by something, maybe, and I can't see anything that hit the truck."

"Maybe," sobbed the girl, "they just hit the truck and took off."

Howe laughed at the thought. "Listen, lady. That was a huge explosion. If something had hit that truck, it wouldn't have been able to drive away."

"I hope nobody was hurt," she answered, tucking her face back into her companion's arm.

("There were people hurt, did you think about that?" asked Paula.

"Of course I did," Howe replied. "What, was I supposed to immediately break into tears? Or rush over and try to put out the fire?"

"You could've tried to help. It would only have improved things for you."

"Yeah, well, I didn't think to, and when Salinas came back out...")

The barber stormed into the street, accompanied by the sound of sirens as the police and fire department screamed onto the scene. He grabbed Howe by the shoulders and pushed him towards the shop. "You fucker, look at this!"

Howe, too stunned to react, tried to sympathize. "Yeah, that's gonna take a lot to clean up."

Salinas slapped him, abruptly, across the face. "Fuck you! You and your 'movement.' You see this? You see this? You never think about who's gonna... " He slapped him again, knocking him to the ground and kicking him in the stomach. Howe lost his breath and began to wheeze, trying to defend himself, to tell Salinas that he was insane, irrational, to no avail. "You bastards," screamed the barber. "You come in here with your coded fucking candy, your shit eating absurd candy. You were waiting for this, weren't you? You're here to make sure it got pulled off!"

"Wha...?" Howe managed, amazed in spite of the hurt, propped himself up on his elbows, slipped for a moment on the glass shards that littered the sidewalk.

"He did disdain the President," shouted the old man to Salinas, stabbing at the air with his cane and winking at the girl. "Did you hear that? He disdained the President. I heard him curse the President." A flock of huge, ungainly crows lighted on a telephone wire across the street, and lined up like barristers.

"I... I didn't," gasped Howe, wondering why he'd bothered buying that box of candy.

"He did," helped the girl, snapping her fingers. "I think somebody should go tell the cops."

"Yeah," said Salinas, unrolling his sleeves and taking a step towards the nearest police car. "Yeah, that's exactly what's going to happen. But first...." Using his sleeve as a glove, he picked up a handful of glass and wiped it across Howe's face, after which he delivered another brutal blow to Howe's head with the sharp and solid point of his penny loafer.

Howe remembered intense pain, then blackness, a hand reaching into his jacket pocket, taking the box of candy. He remembered seeing white, glassy spots, covered in red, seeing Salinas standing next to the black and white car, talking to a uniformed officer, motioning towards him. He remembered being lifted, a agonizing journey on a bed of canvas, the words "head trauma" and "cell." Then a final fuzziness, and, finally, a dark, concrete chamber, ropes, something in his mouth. Then Paula's face, looking over his.

("And here we are," said Paula, motioning for the guard to leave and tightening the bonds that tied him to the chair. The wooden back chafed his neck, the ropes digging into his wrists.

"Here we are," he answered. "I'm still thirsty. Can I have more water? I've only had the one glass today."

"Maybe later," she replied, taking her dark blue jacket off before turning the lights back off. "That's better. I don't want to get stains on my uniform." He felt her calloused and beefy hands run across his chin before delivering another sharp blow to his left ear. "Quite a story, Mr. Howe. And you expect us to believe it?"

"It's the truth," he moaned. "That's what happened. I swear I'm not an Idealist. It's not a crime to dislike the President."

"No, it's not," she replied, laughing. "But it is a crime to talk about it. You're obviously lying, Mr. Howe, and that's not right. But don't worry, you'll come around. They always do." He could just make out her silhouette as she reached down to the floor and hefted up something heavy and rectangular. "In keeping with City Criminal Code, Section 56.4.3, I am officially required to let you know that this is a phone book. It'll bruise, but it won't break the skin."

"That's nice," he said caustically, too weary to care. "But I'd rather you do the job with the latest Sand Quarterly."

"Very funny," she smiled. "I certainly wish we'd met under different circumstances, Mr. Howe. You've been very congenial."

"Always make friends with your torturers. Say, you know what the worst part of this whole affair is?" he asked.

"What's that?"

"That bastard Salinas ever finished cutting my hair."

"Too bad," she said, lifting the phone book over her head and bringing it down in a smooth, calculated motion. "Now, how about you confess?")

5. November 17

"He's trying to explain the concept of death to little girls. Doesn't that make you even slightly curious about his disposition?" Bau leaned over the table with his arms crossed in front of him, his eyes slightly red due to exposure to cigarette smoke, his posture reflecting an intimacy which coalesced before him instead of in him. Lifting his cigarette to his lips without moving anything but his elbow, he took a long drag impartially, having reached the stage in his alcoholic stimulation where every inward breath of smoke anchored him to the table, stopped his swaying for a few moments and targeted his indirection on the scene before him. Bau's thoughts bubbled for a moment. He cursed having allowed himself to get as drunk as this, and then, in an oblique series of images, recalled all of the previous times he'd been so intoxicated, like at Tomas' party the week before when he'd been sick in the yard on an anthill, horrified at the thought that the unsuspecting ants would be drowned in undigested vodka and sausage. Bau remembered a childhood friend whose father would pour molten lead and pewter into anthills, digging out the topological core created when the metal solidified, a silver coral sculpture filled with lifeless ants which was sold to the tourists in the man's souvenir shop, and he unwittingly thought of a similar sculpture made of solid vomit which, according to his dazed condition, looked something like a leafless tree of ambergris. He immediately regretted this recollection as it wandered down and lodged in his stomach, and took another drag from his cigarette in an attempt to suppress this nausea— inducing idea. He realized that his only hope was to continue talking, to continue trying to pass himself off as someone who could still hold his liquor as well as he used to be able to in the Academy. "Doesn't it make you even slightly curious about his disposition? Did I just say that?"

"You did," said Ananda, smiling. "Listen, I think you've had quite enough to drink for one evening. Perhaps we should go for a walk." She began putting on her sweater, something for which Bau had been praying because it meant she was ready to leave soon, and fresh air and movement would surely help him climb out of this haziness.

"You are absolutely correct, my dear," he said. Ananda claimed that he didn't slur his words together when drunk, but he felt otherwise. He felt that his words had to climb a wall of jelly in order to emerge from his lips, and only a few were able to make it over the wall, at which point they were required to swim through a thick and viscous fog to reach the ears of his companions. He saw a glowing but shadowy amoeba of letters, m,y,d,e,a,r, swimming thickly, struggling, from his mouth into Ananda's ears. He stood, slowly, and put on his coat.

"I retain these images that I have when drunk," he said, as they emerged into a night which reminded him of the last snow, even though the last snow was over two years ago. "Whether it be the soft caress of a friend, a falling leaf from an oak lighting on the back of a sleeping dog, the shadow of a little blonde girl playing jacks, the empty purple chairs in the plaza where the old men meet to smoke and play chess and discuss their memories, no matter how dark or sullen."

"Let's go to the plaza, Bau, and sit in those empty chairs," said Ananda, grabbing his hand. "We can pretend we're playing chess, and that we're so old that our dogs are the only ones who recognize us anymore, like Argus and Odysseus." She began pulling him by the hand, then he her, then they began alternating the pull, sometimes quickly, sometimes not, down the street towards the park.

The street sent fleeting and differential modes of perception. Bau knew that he wasn't as drunk as he had been; the cold and the air washed some of the expressive drunkenness from him and opened his eyes a millimeter, the untired and wary millimeter of the premiseless night, a measurement that wasn't wide enough to affect his immediate perception but was just enough to open his filters to the antenna of phenomenon that wandered up and down his body. A paper bag that blew across the street followed them at a happy pace, glad to accompany them, until it was stopped by the carcass of a shark that was directly in the middle of the road. They stopped for a moment to investigate the dead shark, which was split open in the middle like an overripe plantain of blue, the contents of its body spread open and startled by the intrusion. "This is what happens," said Bau, "when the shark dares to venture into the world of man. It gets hit by a car." He giggled.

"Silly," said Ananda. "It probably just fell out of a seafood delivery van."

"Not so, sweetness. Observe." Taking a nearby stick, he spread open the bowels of the animal a bit further, opening the second mouth of the shark which it had not had until so recently. There, amidst the guts of the beast, were the half— digested remains of a squirrel, its belly also split open, a reflection of the lifeless bag which now held its contents. "You see? How is this possible?"

"How did you know that would be there?" asked Ananda, taking a closer look.

"There are some things that one can assume on a night such as tonight. One of those things is that if one finds a dead shark in the road, it will most likely contain the body of a squirrel or another such rodent. Taking this into consideration, I must continue to wonder what we'll stumble across as we continue our journey."

"I wish I had my camera."

"No, if you had your camera, the shark would not have been here. Carrying a camera is one of the quickest and most solidly proven ways to avoid the unexpected. You think the Loch Ness Monster shows itself to people who bring cameras into its murky domain? Never. It would be a tragedy if it were to do so." Bau thought to himself that events that seem to break the laws of space must also break the laws of time, as he believed that the two were inseparable. As cameras do nothing more than freeze time, it would be impossible to actually take a picture of anything out of the ordinary. For this reason Bau never carried a camera, he told her, "unless it is to be used for something mundane, like a drive to the country or a friend's wedding or a trip to another town, where the universe is expected to behave a certain way. I can never remember such insignificant events, and such photographs are only necessary to help one to remember the unmemorable. Cameras tend to be villainous, malcontents, for every camera distorts what it sees, and every photograph is a lie."

"Using that logic," replied Ananda, "every work of art is a lie, too."

"This is true, but some lies are more valid than others."

"I think that stories and books are the real dishonest creations," she replied; Ananda, Bau thought, is the kind of girl who laughs at jokes and then asks you to explain them, not because she didn't get the joke but because she wants an in— depth look at what you think is funny. She continued: "The events that occur in any novel or story are simply ornamental. Like decorations on a great Christmas tree. Accidents. Like a car. The fact that a car happens to be blue, or powerful, or a convertible, is purely accidental. In the same way, a love affair in Proust, a theme of retribution in Shakespeare, these are simply extras designed to make the commonplace seem less so. Every event is a snowball of crystal or a popcorn strand, and eventually the tree has to be taken down and thrown away. Stories, novels, I can't get into them because all of the events that occur seem inconsequential, so impossible. Fiction is simply a decorative art."

Bau didn't know how to respond. Or rather, he knew that he wanted to respond, but the combination of sullen clearness derived from the cold and alcohol running along his synaptic pathways prohibited a coherent response. "Hm," he said, nodding but disagreeing, kicking an errant pebble out of his way.

As they continued towards the plaza, Bau noticed his companion looking over her shoulder every few minutes. "What is it?" he asked.

"I have the strangest feeling that someone is following us. I've felt this way ever since we left the bar. On occasion I think I've caught a glimpse of a giant pink hare behind us, and I feel as though there's been a polarization of the relationship between predator and prey, because I can imagine how a rabbit must feel when he knows he's being stalked by a wolf, and I feel as though I'm being stalked by a malicious rabbit. Let's hurry, okay?"

Bau smirked and passed his arm through the crook of her elbow. "Certainly!" He still found himself unready to craft a reply. A pink rabbit? Nonetheless, he checked over his own shoulder, perhaps creating the strawberry colored streak which stuttered into a nearby alley, perhaps not, but unable to credit the night with the delivery of the dead shark and a predatorial bunny, the accidental events that seemed to accessorize their stroll like a necklace of teeth or a windmill of oars.

A few blocks ahead, under the resonating waves of a black tarpaulin which stretched above a doorway that had succumbed to the temptation of curvature, a number of couples, the remnants of a party that they had passed on their way to the bar, stood chatting in the way that couples chat as the embers of a party are dying down. Bau and Ananda saw Shaker and his fiancée Sarah among the guests, surrounded by the yellowish spillover of the light from inside, and stopped for a moment to chat.

"You bastards missed one hell of a soirée," said Shaker, glowing. "But, Bau, comrade, you still look as drunk as I feel."

"If you think I'm drunk," said Bau, "you should listen to Ananda talk about Christmas tree ornaments, or pink rabbits, or whatever else she's going on and on about." Ananda delivered a sharp blow to his ribs with her elbow.

"I haven't said any such thing," she said. "Bau is as drunk as he usually gets, and he's making things up."

"No, you saw the shark! And the squirrel! You know exactly what kind of night this is."

Shaker laughed. "Shark and squirrel. Sounds pretty intoxicated to me, he does. So what are you kids up to?"

"We're heading to the plaza to sit in the purple chairs and pretend we're playing chess. You two want to come along?"

"No, thanks. We're heading home. It's been a long night."

"Say, what was this party for, anyhow?"

"A dream," said Sarah, who had been drawing obscure

spirals on Shaker's face while muttering about how polluted crop circles made his soul.

"How's that?" asked Ananda.

"Well, you know Antonio, who threw the party? He had this dream the other day while he was taking a nap in a tree. In his dream, he was running through the woods, naked, as is typical in such dreams, being chased by a swarm of winged demons. He could hear his feet crunching on the leaves, feel the parchment between his toes. Finally, he stumbled, and on the ground in front of him he saw a Chaldean symbol carved into a rectangle of wood. He grabbed it, flipped over, and held it up before him. The demons flew off in a rage, unable to harm him."

"So he threw a party?"

"Wouldn't you?"

"Say," asked Shaker, "how did you know that about the dream?"

Sarah smiled and continued to trace the invisible spirals on his face in eyeliner. "Because I was sleeping with him in that tree."

"Oh," said Shaker, kissing her, causing her hand to slip and smear eyeliner along his jawbone.

Bau stumbled under the weight of an impulse. "C'mon," he said, taking Ananda's hand and passing through their friends into the house. "I want to be surrounded by strangers."

Ananda looked over her shoulder and waved goodbye to Shaker and Sarah, who had already left. "What are we doing? We have to get to the plaza! It's starting to become even more important that we do so. I think the rabbit is getting closer!"

"No, no, no. I have to go in here." The room, peppered with

guests, regaled with peacock feathers and powder blue nightgowns, presented very little challenge to them as they weaved through, more than necessary, really, since Bau enjoyed the weaving; he needed to feel as though he was walking down a crowded street, and Ananda wanted to leave but followed him anyhow, because of their friendship. When they reached the kitchen he stopped, they stopped, and he noticed something about the kitchen change, as if he had just entered another dimension where the only difference was that one grain of sand was missing from the beach or one less drop of water fell from the kitchen faucet, kissed her, but she didn't kiss him back.

"Don't do that," she said.

"Of course," he answered. "Of course not."

"Come on." She took his hand and led him back through the party and onto the street. Bau, certain that he'd turn back and see the party guests replaced by what he now perceived as their pink pursuer, glanced over his shoulder and noticed that the black tarpaulin over the door was not black, was actually the dark blue of the ocean reflected on the underside of an approaching storm.

"I don't think it's still behind us," Bau said. "In fact, I'm not sure it ever was. I think you may be imagining things, but if so, then I'm imagining things, too, so."

"So what?"

"Just so."

"I see. Don't worry; it's still behind us. I saw a flash of cotton candy pink just a moment ago."

"And what will it do to us if it catches up to us?"

"I don't know. I can't tell. But that's why it's so important that we reach the plaza. The plaza, it's an oasis for us. We're weary camels being followed by a swarthy and dangerous Bedouin, who happens to be wearing a pink bunny suit."

They stopped talking for the moment; she, tense and worried, had a pensive look, thinking about all kinds of pink rabbits and smiling foxes and the wounded baby flying squirrel she'd found as a child, how she tried to save it, and it had depended on her, trusted her, been fooled into thinking that she was its mother. One afternoon, she forgot to bottle feed it, and it died the following night, found the next morning, its essenceless body coating a dirty white towel in a dirty black shoebox. Upon finding it dead, she realized that she had hoped to turn it into a pet had it lived, was only trying to save it so that she could tame it, that her desire to possess something so frail and protect it had inevitably led to its own destruction. She knew that in this desire, she had let it down, and from that point on in her life she expected to let down the things that loved her, needed her, because she knew she would only destroy them by showing a reciprocal love and need.

Bau, on the other hand, enchanted by the sound of their feet hitting the cobblestones, nodded his head just a bit more with each step, 'clop, clop, clop,' until he seemed to walk like a distended pigeon with an oversized head. Each forward motion he made caused something in his head to glide, the effects of the alcohol no doubt extending the fantastic notion that he could fly, and he thought it would be fun to flap his arms, running ahead, "Coo! Coo! I'm a pigeon!" And damn the accidents that seemed to obfuscate the scenery of his life! Life, pasty and wan, cannot deny a man his right to run down the street cooing like a giant pigeon at two in the morning, and damn the others, damn the torpedoes, damn the obstacles and damn anyone who would die a liar; Bau was an honest man, an honest pigeon, and time to turn around and make it known! "Ananda, back in the kitchen, the kiss, was — "

But she isn't there.

He doesn't think he's run too far, that she was so far back as to be out of sight, so she must have ducked into an alley, and he then remembers that there have been a number of random attacks on strangers to the city; his chin rises and falls, but this time not in the manner of a pigeon, instead looking for his lost companion. He knows she couldn't have disappeared into the sky, but one never knows which direction will prove most successful on an empty street on a cold, snowless night.

Retracing his steps, seeing them etched invisibly on the sidewalk, illuminated by his concern, he reaches the spot where he knows he saw her last. There haven't been any doors in the hundred feet or so, no open windows, no alleys, nothing, and he begins to sweat, feeling the vodka finally making its way out of his pores, not really, but in the same way that one thinks that a car is driving differently after an oil change. "Ananda? Ananda!?" As is traditional, a random dog begins to refute Bau's cries in the distance, and a few lights appear in the top floor windows of the surrounding buildings. Unwilling to admit to himself that a pink hare may have kidnapped his friend, Bau decides she must have run ahead of him to the plaza, and he was so busy pretending to be a pigeon that he missed her, his eyes closed while his arms flapped, more demonically than birdlike, he thinks. Perhaps he came upon an unsealed pocket of time, his flapping arms tracing a pattern in the border that separates us from the place where sharks crawl into the road and eat squirrels, the motions opening a hole into the void, like a medieval magician summoning a spirit, and he banished Ananda into these mists.

Regardless, he decides to continue to the plaza, thinking that she must have run ahead, or, if not, she would head there anyhow knowing he would, and she would wait, alone, wrapping her sweater more tightly around her and shivering in anticipation of his arrival, or the arrival of their pursuer. Walking quite briskly, or, rather, letting the plaza pull itself towards him, he thinks to himself that sometimes events can be disposable, sometimes events can be sold on television or the radio, and sometimes events need to be locked into a safety deposit box and the key thrown away. Although he continues worrying about Ananda, he begins to feel guilty, to think that if she has disappeared, at least he will have a good story to tell his friends, perhaps to write down and have published in fictional form and in the kind of magazines that capitalize on strange disappearances. He certainly doesn't wish her any harm. Maybe she'll turn up years later when he's living in another city, and they'll exchange pleasantries, oh, remember that night you disappeared, you know I wrote a story about it, yes, I actually went home because I was tired and you didn't hear me; he rather felt like someone wondering what his beloved but wealthy grandparents would leave them when they died. But if that were the case, then she'd be married and have children, and he'd still be a bachelor, wondering whether his friend's girlfriends would consent to become involved with him when they'd broken up, or he'd have a long distance friendship with her, one that consisted of phone calls at odd hours due to the time difference and letters that were again simple exchanges of pleasantries and nostalgic recollections of times past like the night she disappeared and he kissed her in the kitchen at a party.

Bau finally smells the roses that bloom in the rose garden next to the plaza. Walking under the steel arch that marks the plaza entrance, he makes his way towards the purple chairs in the center, the original destination, and his pace quickens. He stops only to pick one of the roses, a large pink rose, still in bloom despite the cold, and he notices that as he reaches to pluck the rose from its stem, a blue— white spot appears on one of the petals, a tiny bloom on a larger bloom. He reaches up to touch the spot, and another appears, and a third, until what he sees finally catches up with what he knows, and he looks up and sees that snow dances down from a sky the color of the tarpaulin at the party. He lights a cigarette, and cuts the rose from the stem, taking extra caution to pull his hand into his sleeve so as to avoid getting stuck with thorns. Rose in one hand, cigarette in the other, he continues walking towards the purple chairs.

"Ananda?"

He sees the chess area before him, the snow falling in such a way that the chairs and tables are outlined in white. The chessboards, painted on the tables, begin to transform, shedding their black and white skins and replacing them first with twice as much white as black, and eventually becoming completely white. Bau brushes off one of the purple chairs, sits, wonders how long he'll have to wait before Ananda arrives, and places the rose on the table. The metal chair, like the floor of a meat locker, cools him comfortably, and he remembers at that point that he still has a flask of vodka in his jacket pocket. In the interest of keeping himself warm, he pulls it out and takes a deep swig, the liquid and nicotine causing his heart to jump in his chest.

Accidents, he thinks. Decorations on a tree. Kitchens, pink rabbits, sharks, squirrels, bars, ants, vomit, pewter, silver, gold, sun, warmth, vodka. He takes another swig by association. Psychologists, he thinks, would have a field day with him. Well, he would wait here for Ananda. How dare she simply disappear like that? She knows how concerned he gets about her! With his vodka and this rose to keep him company, Bau would be able to wait as long as it took, and how he would chastise her when she arrived, unless she had a good excuse, which, he supposes, is possible. He hoped she was all right.

The snow seemed to be falling a bit harder; he is no longer able to keep it from accumulating on his lap. No matter. Didn't the Eskimo use snow to keep warm? Well, he would do the same. He would have a blanket of snow and vodka. He took another gulp, feeling acidic and tired, and wondering where she was, because he loves Ananda, pink bunnies aside, and all things aside, so he would wait. Life can't be measured in segments of time or shillings; one has to take the whole thing in. There are no accidents. Everything happens for a reason. Well, not necessarily for a reason, but . . . where the hell is she? He realizes just how sleepy he is, and how she'll be so sorry when she finds him cold and shivering. He'll be able to hold this over her head for so long, especially . . . whew. Another swig of vodka and perhaps a quick nap? Ananda would wake him when she arrived. Yes, that would do him just right. Accidents. He'd show her!

The snowstorm crawled down the sky, each flake spinning down an invisible strand, until six o'clock. When the sun rose in a sky littered with only slivers of clouds, its beams stretched out to caress the overcoat of white which the ground seemed to have put on in order to protect itself from the sun's rays. As the beams danced through the empty plaza, they played tag over the roses, stalks of green, red, and white, and over the playground, which wouldn't be used today, and over the purple chairs, which weren't purple this morning but white, and the chess tables, and when the rays of the sun finally touched the tall, snow covered shape that rested on one of the purple chairs, unmoving, the shape, a round lump on top of another lump on top of the purple chair, turned suddenly and unmistakably cotton candy pink, except for one area about halfway down, where a cotton— candy pink rose petal rested, alone.

6. Bertrand's Last Night Alive

Bertrand stepped onto the number 19 bus at the corner of Grove and Main, just as he had said he would. Sighing, he sighted his customer Ellen in the accordion seat, the midsection of the bus, the hinge that separated the two great, rectangular bodies of the bus, where the two seats faced one another. The accordion section— so called because the plastic hinge that bent and twisted when the bus turned a corner resembled nothing so much as a great concertina— gave Bertrand the willies: the circular floor rotated beneath the seats, producing a feeling akin to a carnival tilt-a- whirl, and his cousin had broken his arm on a tilt- a- whirl once. The ride had been spinning at full force, round and round and round, when suddenly a bolt came loose at the hub of the wheel and the entire contraption plummeted, spinning, twenty feet to the ground. Bertrand shivered, applying this memory to his present situation, and prayed to the Transit Gods that no bolts came off, that the squeezebox section would do him the courtesy of refraining from ripping open, exposing him and Ellen to the harsh asphalt of the street below.

He supposed that Ellen always picked the midsection of the bus to make the exchange because nobody liked to sit there. The two sets of seats, facing one another, always remained empty until the bus was packed full of commuters who had no other options, no other seats to choose from. It seems to be a natural, instinctive fear, thought Bertrand, the fear of riding a bus and having the bus split in two. For this reason, they always sat in the center of the bus to make the trade, and it was always on the Number 19 Bus to the airport at 11:40 PM, the least busy bus of the day; barely any flights left such a small airport after 11:00, so nobody had any reason to go to there, but the bus ran anyhow, serving as nothing more than a mobile office for Bertrand and Ellen's business.

He sat across from her, and she smiled at him. "Hi," she said, with a slight and raspy Oklahoma twang. "Hi, Bertrand." He was sure she'd been pretty at some point, but now she was haggard, thin, with dark crop circles under her eyes, multileveled rings of blue and black, and straggly, thin blonde hair, stringy from too many washes. She had the worn and weary look of the stage actress who leaves the world of theatre to perform in film, but ends up failing miserably in Hollywood and crashing into unknown- ness. She coughed, but her cough was shallow, it reached only into the top of her throat instead of down into her lungs where it would have been had she actually been sick. Although she gave the overall visible impression of relative good health, there was something unkempt about her deepest personal and internal underside, as if peeling back her skin would reveal an elderly, bird- like stick of human butter instead of her psyche; Ellen looked about thirty five, but she radiated a cancerous eighty. "So you have what I need?"

"Right here," he answered, pulling a brown paper bag out of his satchel. His hand grasped the cylinder through the sack, its hard plastic extending its texture underneath the crumpled brown paper, and he gave it a slight shake, enough so that only Ellen or a mother rattlesnake would have detected the skittish sound which emerged, the familiar sound of pill hitting pill hitting plastic. "Look, Ellen, I know this sounds weird coming from me, but I still think it's a waste of your money. I mean, even chemically—"

Ellen's addict smile turned into an addict scowl. "Hey, do I pay you for counseling? No. You're my dealer. So deal." She held out three tens and a five. "This is enough, yeah?" Her voice, sore from forced coughing, cracked and bristled under years of misuse.

He grabbed the cash, counted it, sighed again. "Yeah. Yeah, that's enough." He handed her the paper bag, which she tore into, pulling the bottle out of the side through the bag's wound instead of through the opening at top. Reading the bottle, she exclaimed, "This is the new stuff! 'Mezlocillin,' it says. Hopefully, this'll do the trick. Good job, Bert."

"Thanks," he said. "The pharmacy just got in a new shipment."

"So is it hard to get this stuff away from their prying eyes?" She smiled, opening the bottle and tossing one of the pink pills into her throat.

"Not really," he replied. "Everybody's watching the real drugs. Not many people are addicted to antibiotics, so they're pretty lax about them."

"I'm not addicted, Bert. These are gonna help cure me."

"Cure you? Cure you of what?" The bus lurched around a corner, sweeping Bertrand's feet out from under him, forcing him to grab the leather strap that hung from the wall next to him. "Cure you of nothing? The reason these antibiotics you're taking don't do anything for you is because antibiotics don't work unless there's something for them to fight! You've been through Penicillin, Methycillin, Oxycillin, and seven other different antibiotics, and you're still 'feeling sick.' You've been to eight different doctors, all of whom diagnosed you with the same thing: nothing! There's nothing wrong with you except what's in your head. You need to see a specialist."

She slowly screwed the lid back onto the pill bottle, frowned, and shivered. "You kin say that all you want, because you cain't know. You cain't know what it's like to be sick for months. You cain't possibly imagine what it's like waking up with chills in the middle of the night every night for a week, or having the shits six days out of seven. Ever had a whole week go by where you don't even have a solid shit, Bertrand? Try it, and then tell me that I'm crazy for buyin' antibiotics from you."

"But they don't do anything, Ellen. They can't. It's chemically impossible. In fact, they're probably making you worse. Each antibiotic releases all kinds of crap into your system that's supposed to fight disease. If there's no disease to begin with ... ."

Ellen smiled. "Now, if they make me worse, then they're at least doing something, right? But these do make me feel better, Bertrand, these little pills, be they pink, blue, red, fuck all, whatever, as long as they're antibiotics. I'm sick with something, and someday you're gonna find the drug that'll cure me." She hiked her skirt up an inch, softly whispered, "Bertrand, I know you care about me; you're always so nice. These pills make me feel sooo good. You wanna come back t'my place with me? It's been a long time since I had me a man over." Her fingers stumbled along her thigh revoltingly, as if they had independently managed to catch the diseases that Ellen only thought she had and limped and suffered by their proximity to her legs; they pressed down for a moment on a thick blue vein before leaping across the aisle to pat Bertrand's knee, grab his hand, and pull it towards her. She raised it towards her mouth, just in time to reflexively force a cough, something habitually faked by Ellen to feed her own sense of psychosomatic fullness, and the cough forced out a shower of spittle, which Bertrand couldn't help but feel was colored as pink as the pill she'd popped.

He pulled his hand back, reflexively wiping it on his jeans. "Sorry, Ellen. Look, I can't stand this ride any longer, this accordion section. It gives me the creeps. I'm going to get out at the next stop and cab it back home." He pulled the rubber— coated wire that sounded the stop— bell for the driver.

Ellen stopped her coughing and wiped her own hand on the paper bag. "Damn, well that's too bad. I could make it worth your while, y'know. I may be sick, but that don't make me any worse in bed."

"No, no thanks, Ellen."

"Screw you, then, Bertrand. I was hoping we could get past this dealer/buyer relationship, but you gotta be all business. Then I'll see you next time we have to do business. See you in ... ," she read from the label, "twelve days."

The bus rolled to a stop, screaming and groaning like some long slumbering dragon finally waking up after a century of sleep. Bertrand stood, tipped his hat to Ellen, "Yeah, twelve days or so, maybe," and disembarked, each step down the stairs a step of relief. Ellen hopped up at the word 'maybe' and scooted over to the seat closest to the door so she could pop open the window and shout, "No maybe, Bertrand! I gotta get better! I gotta get my antibiotics, you impotent fuck! I better see you, same time, twelve days, or— " The rest of her sentence was lost in the dull, pregnant roar and echo of the bus pulling away.

He sighed for the third time that evening, and immediately afterwards, he felt a large pressure against him and his ears filled with a sharp squeal as everything went black.

* * *

"Hey, buddy, buddy, you okay?"

Bertrand pried open his eyes, noticed that they seemed glued shut, like he'd fallen asleep with the heat on. The insubstantial oval form leaning over him convalesced into the face of a girl, which pulsed and throbbed. He realized that the face wasn't throbbing on its own; his head, which felt as though it'd been robbed of every pleasant sensation, seemed to cause the shape to jump, blur, move, shake for a solid minute, after which Bertrand finally felt he had found the strength to groan and pass out again.

A constant breeze on his face awakened him once more, and this time when he opened his eyes, he saw great, tall, dark buildings marching by, the occasional offices in the sky rises lit like stars in a monolith. He twisted on leather under his back, or vinyl, something squeaky, and reached his hand to his aching forehead. Finding it coated in a goo of some sort, he held his hand out before him, and, on seeing the dull rusty red that covered his fingers, bolted upright. He immediately regretted having moved, the pain that sparkled in his head moving suddenly down his spine and out of his mouth in the form of a desolate moan.

Sitting back, he saw that he rested in the back seat of a newer model convertible. His hat, by his side, was crumpled and useless, and he chucked it onto the floor. A young woman sat behind the wheel, and she turned around for a moment upon hearing his moan, catching his shadowed movements in her rearview mirror, and he almost moaned again.

She was quite simply the most beautiful woman in the world.

He liked to compare the women in his life to women from Classical Literature. His first girlfriend had been Don Quixote's Dulcinea, his second he called Beatrice. This woman, he thought, should she end up involved with him, would have to be Helen of

Troy. Her hair, stacked loosely on her head, except for two long curls that waved at him in the breeze from in front of each tiny ear, framed a perfectly smooth face, devoid of any flaw. "You're awake," she said, her voice high pitched, but not unpleasantly so. Rather, it was the innocent, unspoiled, high— pitched voice of a girl just past puberty, though she must be in her late twenties, he guessed. He also noticed she had something of an accent; almost British, or Australian, but not very strong.

"Yeah," he groaned. "Hi. You are... excuse me... you are simply the most beautiful person I've ever seen."

"Thanks," she said. "I know."

He held her face in his eye's hands, utterly enchanted. Small, perfect nose. Proportions almost Aristotelian. Da Vinci would have been able to invent entire worlds based on the lines drawn between her features. "What happened?" he asked.

"I hit you," she said. "I was on my way to a friend's house. You got off of the bus and walked into the street as I was making a turn."

"Shit." He felt his forehead again, and found a deep, vaginal gash covered in half- dried blood. "Double shit. This hurts."

"You want something for it?" At the next stoplight, she fumbled around in her glove compartment and handed him two small, white pills. "Valium. Cut with MDMA. I get it made special by a client. Mood altering and pain killing all at once." He took the pills, noticed that her hands were also blemish free, almost as if she had never grown out of her baby skin.

"Where are we going? My name's Bertrand, by the way."

"Amy. Nice to meet you, although it could have happened under better circumstances. Listen, I'll take care of the bills, okay?

We're headed to the Emergency Room. Please don't sue me, though. I can't go back to court."

Sue her? She hit him. She hit him in her car, he thought, or, she hit him on the street with her car, or while he was standing in the street, she drove into him, and she was taking him to the hospital. Yet he'd just as soon hate the sun for burning him, or sue his mother for giving birth to him. "I won't sue you. Look, I don't feel so bad. I think it's just some bruises, this cut on my forehead. Can you just take me home?"

"No way, mister. You need to go to the doctor's, have that stitched up. After, I'll take you home, and, by way of apology, I'll have sex with you. You should lie back, get some rest."

Wha ... what did she say? With his hand still fingering his wound, he gingerly fell back into the seat, the valium kicking in, relaxing him, keeping him from making a rational judgment of her previous statement; he didn't know what to make of anything, only that he felt alternately pleased and puzzled, amazed and brutalized.

A few minutes later, she helped him out of the back seat and into the Emergency Room. Every head in the vicinity turned to look at her, a living collection of cats distracted by a mouse that sat yards away, the regular late night flow of the hospital ER stopped by her presence, or slowed, like a stream that had to cut around a fallen tree. Those who like thin girls saw her as just thin enough, those who like stocky saw her as cherubic and perfectly Reubenesqe, those who prefer blonde marveled at her lush, dishwater blonde hair, while those who liked brunettes thought her light brown hair exquisite.

While waiting in the orange, pastel, hard, smooth plastic chairs of the hospital, she let him rest on her lap, ever so slightly, almost hovering for fear of pressuring her in the wrong way. His head laying on her black dress, her legs crossed, he deliriously fondled her shoelaces with his red— stained fingers, painfully content, slightly hopped up on either the Valium or the Ecstasy, while she brushed her capably smooth hands through his hair, until the rotund and typical night nurse called his name. Amy stood by while the doctor examined him, stitched his wound, declared his injuries nothing more than a mild concussion, and he told the doctor some story about a fall down some stairs, exonerated her, who played the part of a concerned friend who happened to arrive just in the nick of time. By the end of the doctor's examination and stitching, the pills she had given him in the car began to wear off, but his mood remained high as she held his hand softly, carefully, all the way to the car, and they pulled away in the direction of his apartment, across town from the hospital.

And she held his hand, let him rest his head in her lap, joked with him and stroked his hair, obviously had interest in him, and he found himself completely enamored of her. Even though, he thought, she hit me with a car.

On the ride to his place, they began to talk more personally, ask one another about each other. It's like a screwy first date, thought Bertrand, but instead of asking me out, she ran over me. "So what do you do?" he asked her as they rounded a corner.

"I'm a prostitute," she said.

The pain in his head intensified for a moment. "A prostitute?" He clutched at his thoughts, tried to descramble them.

Shit!

So that was her game. His visions, his recollection of the past two hours feel into place, filled all of the empty holes. She's a hooker. Her actions, her attraction to him, they were ... no, he thought. He'd give her the benefit. Perhaps she's a prostitute, but that doesn't change the tenderness with which she treats me, he considered. I'm not very good at reading signals, but I can at least tell if someone's feelings are genuine. "Oh, er—"

"Don't worry, I understand how that comes off," she continued. "It was a conscious decision. I've been a prostitute for five years now, since I was twenty. It's not something I was driven to do by circumstance. I wanted to be a prostitute, ever since I was a little girl."

"You—"

She laughed. "I can tell you're boggled. A typical reaction. But why not? Some people choose to be bankers, some people lawyers, some people— " She motioned at him, signaling that she wanted to know his profession.

"A clerk at a pharmacy. I didn't really choose that. Just kind of happened."

"See, now there's your problem. You're doing something you don't want to do. Me, I know I'm the most beautiful woman in the world. I was Miss Capetown in 1997. I could have gone on to model for fashion magazines, to act, but then people could only look at me. To sing, but then people could only hear me. I could have had a successful career in pornographic films, but then people could only have fantasized about me. I could have done any of that. But I wanted to share my beauty in the most complete way possible, the best way possible, the way that I could literally give of myself as much as possible to as many people as possible. I really had no other choice for a job. Anything else would have been a waste of my god- given possessions."

He nodded painfully, realized as the stitches stretched that he shouldn't be nodding.

"So," she went on, "I moved here and took up selling myself. However, I don't just sell myself, Bertrand. I sell beauty. I share it. I have been given a great gift, the gift of physical perfection. There are many men— and women— who pay nicely for a night where they can possess my beautiful, perfect flawlessness. You should see the look on the face of the man, the ugly little man, who gets to have me for a night, the most beautiful woman ever, and possess me fully, not just a picture like with models. People are so upset with themselves, with their bodies, that they strive to hold onto someone who has no problems, no imperfections. Funny thing, though; most of them do take pictures, so they can show their friends the proof the next day."

"And you're okay with this?" Bertrand began to feel tense and wished the ecstasy hadn't worn off so quickly.

"Okay with it? I encourage it!" She laughed again. "What other woman in this city, or even in this country, gets to make so many people so happy, gets to share perfection with the less fortunate. And then gets to be shown around in offices, subways, homes, apartments. It's a different kind of fame I'm after, a different kind I have."

Bertrand's mind reeled. "Then I have to ask you. Earlier, did you say you'd sleep with me? I mean—"

"Oh, sure. I did you a bad turn, and you did me a good turn by not getting me in trouble for this little accident, so the least I can do is repay you with myself. Free of charge, of course. Don't you think I'm beautiful? Of course you do, you said so earlier. Is that enough for you?" She placed his hand on her downy thigh, pushed up her dress, mirrored what Ellen had done earlier, and Bertrand's fingers curled at the touch of her tender, velvet skin, the thought of what his fingers could pursue if they wanted to slide about a foot more in the right direction. He jerked his hand away again, sadly, he thought, just like with that sick hypochondriac, the clutter in his brain forcing his digits from moving further up Amy's leg until he knew more.

"No, that's ... that's nice of you. Look, you are, simply, the most beautiful woman in probably the world— "

"There's no probably about it, Bertrand. You are a lucky man."

"Yes, yes. And I appreciate the offer, it's very kind. But I have to know ... ." He paused, thinking of resting on her lap in the waiting room, the caress of her fingertips against the rim of his ear. He closed his eyes and shuddered deeply.

"Yes?" she asked, skimming her hand down his shoulder and arm.

"Well, I have to know if you have stronger feelings for me than ... than what you have for your 'customers.' I mean, in the Emergency Room, and the holding hands, and..." He noticed she was trying to stifle a giggle, and his head throbbed again. "I see. It was nothing, then."

"No, Bertrand!" She stopped giggling and pouted, her thick lips downturned. "It's not like that. I treat all you men with perfect tenderness. It's what I do. It's not that I don't have these feelings for you, it's that I do have these feelings for everyone. I'm in love with every person in the world, Bertrand. Not just one. I am perfect fairness. Isn't this the place?" They had pulled up in front of his apartment building, stopped in front of the stoop, and he reached out, opened the car door, stepped out as she turned off the engine. She exited the car as well, walked around to where he stood, thinking, his head bowed between his hands. "Well? Are you going to ask me upstairs?"

He leaned up against the cold metal pole holding up a striped tarp above the door, let a quiet whistle escape his teeth. "One more thing. What do you usually ask for ... you know, for a job?"

She tilted her head slightly to the left, frowned. "Why do you ask?"

"Curious."

"Oh. Hm. Well, it depends from person to person. The going rate is fifty for a quickie, more than that is a hundred an hour. But if someone can't pay, I'll usually ask for something more minimal. A foot massage. A meal. Whatever."

He pulled three crumpled ten dollar bills, the ones Ellen had given him, from his pocket, wadded tightly in his fist. With an underhand toss, he plunked the wad of cash into her back seat. "That's thirty," he said. "Since you hit me, I'm keeping the other twenty."

"Oh, but you don't have to— " she reached out and touched his arm.

"No," he interrupted. "You don't understand. I'm not paying you to come upstairs and fuck me, as much as I'd enjoy that. I'm paying you to get in your car and drive away."

The soft look on her face turned into a look of exquisite horror. "You're turning me down? But I owe you!"

"You gave me two hours of happiness. For two hours I thought you had a thing for me, a crush on me or something, for two hours. For two long hours of my life, from the time you gave me the pill until you told me you were a prostitute and then explained your fucked up reasoning behind your career choice. Look, Amy. I really like you, really, and I don't think you could ever value that, and I think that if we were to go upstairs and spend even a half hour together, I'd just get deeper and deeper into you, and then you'd wake up and go fuck some guys just to make them happy while I'd sit at home thinking about what I'd just had and could never have again without paying for it, and even then, never exclusively. Your world— view is funky, Amy. I know I kept you from some business tonight, so that's what the thirty bucks are for. Now please get out of here."

Angrily, with faint traces of tears in her eyes, just a touch of wetness that could just as well have come from driving with the top down, Amy stormed around to the other side of her car, wordlessly, opened the door, sat down, started the engine, looked over her shoulder, said "You could have had me but turned me down. Nobody's ever done that. You missed your one chance at true happiness, asshole!" She threw the money back at Bertrand, where it hit his chest and bounced off. Spinning her tires in a puddle, she tore off, leaves and dust tossed up into the air behind her.

Bertrand reached down, picked up his money, and a sharp pain rippled through his head. He stuffed the wad of bills into his shirt pocket, pulled his keys out, and ever so softly and sadly, stepped into his building.

* * *

Bertrand decided that it would be best if he tried to forget about Amy and pick up his next "delivery" from his room. In the entryway to his building, the blue stained carpet, which looked something like a shag rug that had been mowed down to the floor, squelched beneath his shoes, perpetually wet with an indiscernible and undiscovered leak. It produced a mildewy scent, the smell one would imagine contained in the spaces between the spores of a dust cloud. He always smiled at the look of the wallpaper; although peeling slightly, it still retained something of a Jazz Era charm, depicting sleek black panthers in art deco poses amidst golden fleur- de-lis. On each of the posts on either side of the tapered stairs, a dim, candle shaped bulb gave off a fuzzy yellow glow.

As he passed his landlord's door, the first door on the right, the rank, banana- like odor of the carpet caused Bertrand to sneeze, his head drawing back and a great blast erupting from his nose that caused intense needle- sharp pain to run through his head injury. Becoming dizzy for a moment, Bertrand rested his hand on the thick, wooden door to wait for the waves of pain to subside. The wood felt like hard leather: bumped, grainy, smell a little like leather stain, and he imagined a great sheet of cow skin being formed into a door through a long process of curing. This led immediately to speculation on who would do such curing; who would make doors out of leather? Dwarves? Gnomes? As the gnomes frolicked with their leather curing equipment in his head, the door gave way beneath his palm and swung inward at the command of his landlord, Mr. Palvey. "Bertrand, am I glad to see you," the landlord said in his striking baritone, removing his hand from the knob and wiping a sheen of sweat from his bald head.

"Hi, Mr. Palvey," said Bertrand, standing upright. "How's the arm treating you this evening?" Palvey's right arm had been bandaged and in a sling since Bertrand had moved in two months ago, the result of an undisclosed injury.

"Oh, they're fine, they're fine," Palvey answered. Bertrand could detect the faint and raw scent of alcohol on Palvey's breath, and noticed a blanket of what seemed to be dew on the man's full beard. "Sorry to bother you this late, just coming in and all, but I wonder if you could give me a hand with something? I need some help opening a jar. One good arm and all, you know."

Although Bertrand felt as though his head was going to burst open like an overripe piñata, he agreed to accompany Palvey into his apartment to open the jar. He'd always been slightly intimidated by Palvey, who stood a few inches above most men he knew, and figured that getting on the landlord's good side was always worth a few minutes of doing something he didn't necessarily want to do. He made his way into the apartment behind Palvey and summarily found himself breathing through his mouth as the smell intensified. Apparently, Palvey had a veritable zoo of house pets living in his two room suite. Bertrand counted an anxious and spotted Corgi bounding over the orange and blue matted couch and yipping, three identical grey cats which sulked and purred in and out of his legs like a driver's ed student in a traffic cone obstacle course, and what seemed to be a small flock of sparrows that flew in short circles around the spider- covered chandelier. "Ah, you have animals," he commented through the cloud of pet dander and flea shampoo.

"Yup," said Palvey. "This here's my little family. The dog's Leopold, the four cats are Berthe, Suky, and Merlin, and Hilda's probably hiding under the couch there, and the birds, well, they don't have names, really. Not like you can call a sparrow and have it come to you. They just came in one day and decided to stick around. Oh, and up there on the lights, that's Esmerelda and Santiago." It took a moment for Bertrand to realize that Esmerelda and Santiago were two fat, black, shiny spiders.

Palvey seemed to take wonderful care of his menagerie, all things considered. The odor didn't strike Bertrand as an offensive, fecal odor, the kind that hangs about in bathrooms and closets that house litter boxes in urban hipster apartments. Rather, it smelled as if the entire herd of beasts received a flea dip on a daily basis; it was a deep, rich, medicinal smell, like in a dog groomer's shop he used to hang around as a kid, but stronger. The living room contained said couch, a small television set with a coat- hanger and tin foil antenna, and a simple lamp, as well as two worn and scuffed scratching posts and a few cat toys. The lack of a mess made Bertrand wonder if Palvey spent his entire day cleaning up after his pets, taking a rest for five minutes, and then cleaning up after his pets again, the kind of clockwork schedule that he'd have to maintain in order to keep his apartment so spotless with this many animals around. Bertrand also wondered if the man ever had a chance to sleep.

"The jar's here in the kitchen," said Palvey, ducking under a birdfeeder that hung like mistletoe from the arch separating the two rooms. If you get kissed under mistletoe, thought Bertrand, then what happens under a birdfeeder? "I really appreciate your coming by," continued the landlord. "Fact is, whenever I get drinky, I get the biggest hankering for some pickled okra. You ever have pickled okra? No? Well let me tell you that this is the best flavor you'll ever experience. You want a drink or somethin'? I got a fresh bottle of rum." He opened a bottle and poured himself a shot, sucking it down with a slurp as if it was some glass, alcohol filled oyster.

"I'm fine," answered Bertrand, trying to dance around the cats underfoot. "I actually can't stay." The kitchen, tidy and shiny, struck Bertrand as fairly typical, but containers of animal feed covered every square inch of counter space. He noticed a mason—jar full of okra on the counter next to the refrigerator; it looked like a jar of slotted green Frankenstein fingers soaking in a thin, brown fluid. "Is this the jar you need opened?"

"Yup, Bertrand. Yup it is. You ever have pickled okra? Did I ask you that already? You'll have to excuse me, I'm a little pickled m'self."

"You sure did," answered Bertrand, lifting the jar from the counter. "No problem. Let me just ... ." The metal lid on the mason jar had a few brown rust spots on its surface, and he wondered aloud where Palvey managed to find pickled okra in this climate.

"Oh, I have some around from when I used to live in the Ozarks. You ever been to the Ozarks, Bertrand?"

"I sure haven't," said Bertrand, wondering how long ago Palvey lived in the Ozarks and how long ago this jar of okra had been pickled.

"S'a damn shame. You should go there sometime. Beautiful people." He took another shot of rum. "B'tiful people down there."

The landlord was beginning to slur his words. "Best people in th' world come from th' Ozarks. Most hospit'ble people in th' world. S'where I learned t'be hospitable, Bertr'nd. S'where I learned to take care of things."

"Oh, yeah?" Bertrand replied, hoping he wasn't about to get sucked in. Trying to change the subject, he felt for the thirty five dollars in his shirt pocket. "Hey, I have an advance on some of next month's rent for you if you— "

"Whassat? Rent? Nah, don't worry 'bout that now. Just open th' jar."

Bertrand shrugged and left the cash in his pocket. With a loud shlurp, he twisted the lid off the jar.

"Hey!" screamed the landlord. "You did it! Y'see, I tol' you you could do it. He did it, Leo," he said, addressing the dog. "All you animals liss'n! Bertr'nd opened the jar! We have okra! Bertr'nd you're a good guy, y'know? A really good guy." He poured another shot of rum into his mouth. "Y'know what? Bertr'nd, I want to intr'duce you to some folks. Would y'like that?"

"Well," replied Bertrand, "I really should be going. Perhaps— "

"Nonsense! Right now, I say," bellowed Palvey.

Slightly ill at ease, Bertrand decided to humor the man for a few more minutes. Maybe he's just lonely, he thought, and needs someone to talk to. "All right, I'll hang around until they get here, but then I have to get going."

"That's th' spirit!" said Palvey, slurping down an entire piece of okra. "Wait, until th'y get here? But they're already here, m'man. Tell you what, you go ahead and take a seat on th' couch, just brush the cats off, and take a seat. Have some okra." He held the jar out towards Bertrand.

"No, that's— "

"No, have some okra."

Obligingly, Bertrand reached into the lukewarm fluid and withdrew a long stalk of okra, nibbled the end. It tasted like a salty olive, and he decided to take in the whole thing at once in order to get done with it as quickly as possible. Following Palvey's lead, the landlord staring at him intently the whole time, he slurped the pod down into his throat. When he realized that it was covered in tiny hairs, he gagged, and bit down, chewed the skin as much as possible and swallowed the tiny, round seeds whole.

"That's it, there y'go," said Palvey affectionately. "Now you go sit down, and I'll be right back." He exited through a door, behind which Bertrand made out the fluorescent lights of a bathroom.

Taking a seat on the couch, surprisingly comfortable despite its appearance, Bertrand allowed one of the cats to climb onto his lap and began stroking it, watching the sparrows spiral back and forth around the light fixture. With a graceful swoop, one of the tiny birds pounced on a spider, swallowing it whole, and Bertrand wondered which spider it was, Esmerelda or Santiago, that had met such an untimely demise. While he was wondering at the time, the bathroom door squeaked open and Palvey's voice entered the room ahead of the landlord himself.

"Y'see, m'friend, I am a landlord by choice." He stepped into sight, his once— bound arm unwrapped and out of the sling. "It strikes me, and th's may be the Oza'k hospitatily speaking, that nothing should be without a home. So I have me my tenantshere, in th's fine, big, b'lding, you and Steve in 8— B and Ella 'nd the rest, and I have me m'arm tenants, n' I take good care of y'all, so ... meet m'tenants." Palvey thrust his arm under Bertrand's nose, and

Bertrand grimaced in shock while the landlord rattled off a list of names, none of which Bertrand actually heard.

Palvey's arm, now giving off the aroma of rotten meat, swarmed with a white tangle of thick, fat, healthy maggots. As Bertrand watched, his head spinning, unable to take his eyes off of the decrepit and swollen limb, one of the worms that had recently matured into a hairy black fly flew off towards the ceiling and was caught in the spider's web on the chandelier. "Oop, looks like Howard's all grown up and on his own now," said Palvey, ignoring the fly's death.

Underneath the thick layer of living and squirming life soaked a great pool of pus, upon which the seething mass fed. "Mr. Palvey, that's ... that's terribly unhealthy," he found himself saying, wondering what else it was that he could possibly say without risking the offense of his landlord.

"Nah, s'not, s'not unhealthy. S'clean. They eat th'rot, y'know, and I clean it, clean around 'em. They have to have someplace to go, right? They don't know n'better. So I gotta take care of'm, like I take care o'you, and of Steve, and Ella, and all my ten'nts. Well, I guess I'm go put the dressin' back on 'em. Won't do to have any more of 'em leave like Howard did." Palvey wordlessly, maternally, cooed to the maggots as he shambled back to the bathroom.

Bertrand decided it was time to go.

Pushing the cat off his lap and dodging the stub legged Corgi, he made his way to the door. "I have to go, Mr. Palvey, and thanks for the okra," he called, hoping to get out while the man was still dressing his 'other tenants.' Shuddering at the taste of salt and ammonia in his mouth, and the combination of experiences and ingestents making him nauseous, he turned the knob and opened the door. As he glimpsed the light of the hall, the mysterious fourth cat bolted from under the couch and out the door, a galloping streak of grey fur. "Shit," thought Bertrand, "that cat doesn't have a collar on. Dammit!"

He closed the door and decided he'd better go after the beast.

Tonight was not turning out the way he'd hoped it would.

* * *

It took him a moment to remember the cat's name. "Hilda," he whispered. "Hilda!" He cupped his hands to his mouth and clucked after the cat. "Here, kitty kitty kitty!" At the corner of the building, he saw Hilda, shivering, staring at him with wide, green eyes. He crouched down and held out his hand, wished he had some cat food or catnip or something. "Come here, girl. Come on."

Hilda stared at his hand for a moment, sniffed, meowed. With a small jerk, she spotted something in the alley next to the building and crouched. The cat leapt into the alley, and Bertrand stood, grumbling, and began walking, calling after the feline. He stopped at the entrance of the alley, scanning, unable to make out anything but vague shapes in the dark corridor. He broke the scene into sections, scanned each one for movement, all the while calling after the cat. After straining his eyes for a moment, he saw movement to the right near a stack of beat- up aluminum garbage cans, and two green eyes, set on high- beam, appeared, giving him enough of a reference point to make out Hilda's shape. "There you are! C'mon, Hilda. I have things to do and one of them is to get you back to your nutso owner, so let's make this easy, okay?"

He moved slowly, trying to avoid sudden moves that might scare the beast away. With a short leap, he reached out and had the cat's tail in his hand. "RrOWW!" Hilda, demonic and hissing, twisted around and slashed his arm, sending climbing pea shoots of pain up his limb and into his shoulder. "Shit!" he screamed, as he plummeted into the trash cans and knocked them over, creating a symphony of crashes and bangs. Hilda bulleted further into the alley and Bertrand stood, righted the cans, wondered if he shouldn't just let the damned thing go. Although he couldn't make out the depth of the scratches on his arm, he felt that they were relatively deep, and his fingers came back coated in a thin, sticky layer, the second time tonight that he identified his own blood by touch.

The alley erupted with two great "POP!"s and a yowl. Bertrand jumped, startled, images flitting through his head like an old time nickel peepshow; he wondered why a giant would be making huge popcorn in an alley so late at night, who could have driven a car with bad tires into such a small alley, whether or not he should run, landed on the image of a gun being fired and stopped there. It had definitely been the sound of a gun— a small pistol most likely— and the yowl ... damn and double damn. "Hilda?" he squeaked, as quietly as possible, questioning his own stupidity, and standing on the balls of his feet, ready to scatter at the slightest hint of movement. If someone wanted to rob him, he thought, they'd only get the thirty five dollars he'd received from Ellen. Which probably meant that they'd be upset that he carried so little cash and plug him, twice, in the head, he thought, another two pops that some other passerby would think about for a split second before realizing that some nut job was in the alley shooting people. Not that that would surprise him; he'd already been hit by a car and mauled by an animal tonight. If, on the other hand, this mysterious pistolman just decided to shoot the cat, then Bertrand would have to collect the corpse and take it back in to drunk, insane Mr. Palvey, who would most likely evict him for being an inadvertent cat murderer, "Ozark hospitality" notwithstanding.

Bertrand shuffled tiny steps forward into the alley, looking for the cat and the gunman, two different kinds of expectation, one for his own life and one for Hilda's, and tried not to make any sound, lest he reveal his location to the invisible assailant. Ahead in the barely developing fog, he could just make out a square of light from a window, offset by a figure which was leaning over Hilda's body, or corpse, as the case may be. The light softened every few seconds and grew brighter, something in the window interrupting the flow of protons that showered into the alley. "Hey," he shouted, feeling dangerous and resigned. "Hey, I ... I have a cell phone and my finger is on 911," he shouted, thinking quickly to shove his hand into his pocket to fake the phone and wincing as pain rushed through the scars the poor cat had left, possibly its last malicious act in a surely maliciously lived life.

The figure in the light looked up, and held up his gun— free hands. Bertrand began to relax when he saw that the figure was just a standard, garden— variety bum, or hobo, unshaven, with a clichéd red bandana, no doubt filled with sundries like beans, and pocketknives to trade with young, suit— wearing, precocious kids from 1930's double features. This pole/bandana outfit was propped against the wall next to the window, and it began to slide down along the bricks. The bum reached out to steady it, looked at Bertrand and growled in a voice that Bertrand thought was the voice of all hobos: "That 'nine' part isn't true, is it?"

"Nine?" Bertrand wondered if he'd been wrong this whole time, that 911 should be 411 and vice— versa. He'd never used 911 before. Was he wrong? Was it 911, or was it something else? "I'm sorry?"

"Nine lives," said the hobo, pointing down to the cat. Bertrand's mental refrigerator light blinked on. "Oh, the cat. Poor thing. It belongs to my landlord." He began to walk towards the corpse, hoping for incorrectness in calling it a corpse before checking it. "Did you see who shot it?"

"Sure did. I shot the little fucker."

Bertrand stopped walking, just at the moment when he

could turn his head to the left and look over at the heavily frosted window in the wall, and see into the building; the shadows in the rhombus shaped light that Hilda's body rested in were being made by— — what seemed to be— — a tall, thin man chopping, with an axe, something on the floor inside the apartment. "Thp, thp, thp," went the axe, its 'chop' dulled by the glass, each slice through the air producing a grey blink of un— light in the alley. "You ... shot the cat?"

As if to reply, the bum pointed his gnarled hand towards a pile of grey and red on the floor of the alley, a pile which lolled for a moment, just out of reach of the cat's body. "The shitter killed that there rat," he said, gravelly. "Don't much care for things that kill rats."

Bertrand blinked, took his hand out of his pocket. It's time, he thought, to get the fuck out of here. "Well," he stuttered, "I can understand your logic. I mean— "

"Wassat your cat?" asked the bum, producing a small but necrotic looking pistol.

"No, no sir," said Bertrand. "I was just trying to return it to its owner, who— "

"'S a good thing, for sure. For certain, mister! I can't abide cats or cat owners. They're too much of a threat."

"Oh, sure, sure." Bertrand had passed the point of trying to understand the madman, and now chartered scenarios like cruises in his head, looking for one that would allow him to leave the alley without getting shot in the back. Now was not the time to begin questioning the malign logic of a swarthy, rat— loving maniac. "I know what you're saying, man."

"Yeah? They're too much of a threat for me 'n my pal here." Reaching into his tied red and white bandana, he tenderly removed a struggling white form, which he flaunted towards Bertrand. "This here's my pal. My only pal on the street. Now, I know you're thinkin' that I'm some maniac, out here killin' cats just 'cause my mind is so short on fluids that it can't tell the difference tween a cat and some fucker who wants to steal my stuff, but that ain't the case, y'see? So look at this and tell me I'm some maniac, partner." Stepping towards Bertrand, gun still at the ready, he thrust the form— a great, fat, white, pink— toed, red— eyed rat— directly under his own nose, and sniffed, snorted, inhaled. "This is the smell of friendship. You ever had a friendship so pure you could smell it?" He shoved the rat at Bertrand's face. "Try it. Smell that there friendship."

Bertrand took a small sniff, as if a tiny bit of mucous sat in his nose, winced at an unrecognizable smell, a mixture of rat and garbage and, for some reason, vanilla, that stained its patchy and mottled fur. "Oh, imagine that. I can certainly smell that he's a great friend of yours. I can see why you'd want to kill cats who might hurt him."

The bum removed the rodent, grinned, squinted with his left eye. He stepped away and lowered the pistol. "You know what, you're all right. And now you can see why I killed that shitter there. Fucker. Without young Bertrand here, I'd have nobody t'keep my company out here."

Bertrand backed up a step. "Bertrand?"

"Thas his name. Named by m'graddaughter, who gifted me with young Bertrand 'bout, oh, a year ago. Y'ever met my granddaughter?"

Something's not right here, thought Bertrand. Is this some kind of horrible joke? Did his landlord and his crazed hobo friend plan this entire affair, deciding that the culmination would be the rat named Bertrand? Was it some sort of revenge trip? Did he owe anyone money? "That's very interesting," he replied. "My name is Bertrand, too."

The bum looked at him askance. "No shit, really? Nah, yer fuckin' with me. Nobody's named Bertrand anymore. Last Bertrand I knew died durin' the war. Had his chest blown wide open by one of them whatchacallits— "Idealists" or some shit. Fuckers. He was a bud of mine." A drop of moisture appeared in the bum's left eye as he finally put his pistol into his bandana with the rest of his belongings. "Crazy thing is, m' granddaughter didn't even know him, but she named this fella after him anyhow. So I cain't imagine yer name's actually Bertrand, buddy. Nosiree."

Bertrand tossed his hands up in sheer exasperation. "You're right. I was kidding with you— joshing you. My name is actually Percival. Seen a golden cup around here anywhere?"

The bum ignored his question, lovingly stroking Bertrand the Rat. With a sigh of, "Ah, Bertrand, what're we to do?" he sank to the ground under the window, the chop— chop— chop of the axe wielder behind the Venetian Blinds casting a prison cell of shadows across him. With each "chop," Bertrand took a step backwards, keeping his eye on the bum, making sure he didn't zap into his pack and unleash the gun, but the man was too busy entertaining his furry companion to notice Bertrand's exit.

* * *

Ordinarily, Bertrand thought to himself as he neared his friend Bau's house an hour later, it would be time for bed. He climbed the white, marble stairs that led to the front door of the three story Victorian Mansion, patting the head of one of the two lion statues which surmounted the porch. If that bum was here, he wondered, would he blast the fuck out of these lions? Does the bum have the same problems with lions that he does with other cats?

Entertaining himself with visions of lions eating rats and

lions eating hobos, Bertrand rang the buzzer. A few moments later, Bau came to the door, his torso wrapped in a towel but otherwise completely naked. "Hey, Bert! How are you, my friend?"

"Hey, Bau. Did I come at a bad time?"

"No, no! Come right in. I was expecting you. Good old reliable Bertrand. 'Sides, ain't like you've never seen me unclad before. I have some company this evening, so you'll have to excuse the mess. We've been here for the last four hours with some great shit that Santos brought back from Greece. He's from there. Well, I think he is. I'm really not sure." Bertrand followed his friend through the dark hall, running his hands along the horizontal lines that separated the planks in the wall, feeling the slightly crusty texture of the plaster between the boards. As they approached the sitting room, he added another smell to the collection of odors he'd been experiencing this evening. It wasn't quite pot; he knew how pot smelled. And it wasn't quite hash, either— hash smells like pot, but stronger. Rather, the smell permeated into the sinuses like eucalyptus; it was almost minty, and the smoke that hung low in the air seemed heavier than it should have. He noticed that the thick coils hovered through the atmosphere at neck level instead of wading towards the ceiling, and in the light of the dim, arrow-shaped bulbs of the black iron sconces in the wall created a pool of grey- blue eels of smoke which swam about, coiled themselves around his neck.

The living room floor, covered in cushions, reminded him of an opium den from some Sixties Western film, set in Chinatown. Or, better yet, more like the palace of an errant, kingdomless Shah from The Arabian Nights who expects a genii to deliver a princess at an appointed hour. The cushions, embroidered and tasseled, stretched from wall to wall, and smoke sheathed each one in a halo of blue. "Bertrand, have you met Santos?" asked Bau, motioning towards a swarthy, mustachioed gentleman with sparkling eyes who rested prone on one of the cushions.

Twisting his moustache like a Turkish Agha, Santos stood, extended his hand towards Bertrand. "Hello, my friend."

"Nice to meet you," said Bertrand, moving towards Santos, stepping lightly so as not to ruin the silk pillows. They shook hands; or, rather, Santos palmed Bertrand's hand with his great mitt. Looking down as Santos grabbed for a pipe full of the 'herb du jour,' Bertrand noticed a peacock feather tattooed on each of the Greek's fingers.

Santos noticed Bertrand looking at his skin, grinned, took a deep puff from the pipe, and began to speak in a hypnotically deep but nearly silent voice as he exhaled, and Bertrand, perhaps, he thought, from a contact high, thought he could make out a dark parade of images in the smoke. "One night in Uayeb, a city in my homeland," began Santos, "when the Bird of Night had spread its wings over the City of Wanderers and the Priests of the Dog shambled through the streets, the angel Tzadkiel appeared before the Prince of that city and commanded the young man to extend his hands before him. When the Prince's hands were outstretched, the angel stepped forward and gestured, and on the young man's hands appeared the brilliant blue— green feathers of the peacock; on each finger was tattooed a single feather, each of exceeding detail and delicacy, each consisting of exactly one thousand and sixteen intertwined strands of lapis blue and olive green. Each of his nails was stained with the feather's eye, a golden halo surrounding a blackened disc, and no amount of polish or cutting could remove the eye from its nail. It is said that the angel had no words for the Prince, for what use are words in an indescribable situation, and what further messages could Tzadkiel have had for him? Were the feathers not enough?"

Bertrand blinked. "Feathers?" Santos broke the atmosphere with a deep laugh and blew the rest of the smoke from his lungs into Bertrand's face.

"Hey, Santos," said Bau, "spark old Bert here up if he wants in on some. I have business to attend to. Oh, and I gotta get your money, Bert. Did you bring the stuff?"

"Yeah, right here," replied Bertrand, patting the three pills that rested in his pants pocket.

"Cool. Back in a flash or two." He exited the room, scratching his left leg under the towel.

Bertrand took a rather uncomfortable seat on a tubeworm shaped pillow next to the large Greek, crushing the midsection of the pillow against the floor, which felt like hardwood. He noticed Santos leering at him, grinned self— consciously, wondered when the hell Bau would be back down and who his friend was balling. "So what are you smoking?" he asked the Greek. "Bau says you brought it back from Greece?"

Santos coughed, each hack bringing another cloud of powder— blue smoke up from his depths which spread through the air like spores of snow. "No, no, not Greece," he answered in a thick, indiscernible, vaguely Mediterranean accent laden with cooked meat, whole wheat pita bread, and vanilla. "I don't come from nowhere."

Bertrand noticed that a ball of some waxy substance lurked between the erstwhile Greek's thick, sore— covered lips, a substance that Santos munched upon whenever not smoking. He must be chewing a vanilla candle, thought Bertrand, picturing the man, tattooed hands and all, buying a bag of vanilla candles from a shocked, sixty year old woman at the corner drugstore. "So do you mind if I ask where you come from?"

"No, I don't mind. Go ahead and ask." For some reason, Santos found his reply hilarious, and proceeded to laugh at a ridiculous volume.

Bertrand hated situations like this, and Bau always did this to him, left him alone with some crazy with alien drugs. He felt like a nudist in a retirement home, or more like a disguised cow in a gaucho's tent, trying to moo along with the tangos, and he didn't care where Santos came from; he just wanted his money so he could replace his landlord's cat the next morning. Or, he supposed, this morning. After all, it was already past two. He closed his eyes and listened to the warbling of the bluebird of his thoughts; they figured that Santos must be the anti— Santa: fat, creepy, living at the South Pole, and instead of looking forward to his visit, little boys and girls curl up with fear at the voluminous sound of his hack— hacking. And instead of reindeer, he had a sled pulled by huge, black peacocks, crying through the stars and shouting, "you want to know what this is I smoke and your friends smoke?"

He opened his eyes, realized the man had actually asked this last question. Dizzy, he sat up further, moved to an unsquashed area of the pillow. "Sure, sure. What is that you're smoking?"

"I hear you can deal things, no?"

"Yeah, I do that on occasion." He sighed, wondering at the marketability of such an odd plant, foreseeing complaint after complaint about the nasty trips it must give you.

"Yeah, yourself. Well!" Santos shouted. "You want to sell this! I'll tell you what it is. But you can't tell nobody, okay? I tell you because I like your friend, he is good to me and lets me stay here." He leaned over, closer and closer, until the sound of his eternal chewing created a rhythm, chew, chew, chew, that reminded Bertrand of an Italian funeral march, tubas and the Virgin Mary. "It's from babies," he whispered, releasing a mist of vanilla into the air.

Bertrand couldn't help but scoff, tried to turn his outburst into a forced cough. "Babies, huh?"

Santos sat back. "Yes, babies," he solemnly replied. "In my country, there is a bad problem. You know, all the women like to do the drugs." He pronounced it "dorogs." "And they do the drugs while they are, you know, pregnant. And the babies are born, and they are born hooked, because they have so many drugs that were in them from their mothers. And you take these babies, and when they are, say, done, you can find in them, in their tiny brains, a great combination of drugs. So this is how you make this. It's a powder. Powdered baby brains." He giggled girlishly, outlandishly.

"Baby brains?" asked Bertrand, appalled. "And where do you get these baby brains?"

Santos grinned and spat a ball of white into his hand, which he placed into a handkerchief. He wiped his hand on Bertrand's pillow. "I find them, see. They can be found."

"So you buy them?" Is this some sick black market thing, he thought, starting to wonder at the man's veracity.

"No, no, I don't buy them. I make the drug myself. It was MY idea, see, nobody else's." He moved towards Bertrand again, a bit more belligerently. "This is why I don't tell nobody. You know, I look for someone to sell these, and nobody will! This is why I tell you. You want in?"

Bertrand thought for a moment, repulsed. "So ... you ... you kill babies? And make drugs out of their brains? Is that what you're saying?"

"My friend, you make it sound so bad. But it's not bad; it's better than the life these babies would live otherwise. You know what I think? I think what I'm doing is ... how do you say, when you make a metal more pure— "

"Refined?"

"Yes, yes! I am refining these babies. I am taking their perishable little flesh, and taking the spirit, and the spirit is taken into everyone who smokes from Santos's pipe, you see?"

Bertrand began questioning the other man's motives. Is he telling me this to freak me out? This can't be serious. He's fucking with me. No way. If he's fucking with me, I should just play along, right? But if he's not fucking with me... no, he has to be fucking with me. Okay, I'm game. "Well," he finally replied, "I'd better try these 'baby brains,' before I decide whether or not to act as your distributor, shouldn't I?"

The ex- Greek laughed. "Now you're talking, Bert!" He reached for the pipe, grabbed the slim, blue glass neck as if it was an intimidating swan that needed strangling, and loaded the bowl with a pinch of powder from a brown paper bag. He passed the pipe and a lighter to Bertrand, who proceeded to light and inhale.

He immediately noticed how hard it was to take a hit, like trying to suck liquid through a drinking straw full of paper. The strong inhalant made him cough, and felt as though someone had force fed him a ball of steel wool, and the strength of the smoke as he exhaled measured up pitiably next to the smoke that trickled out between Santos's teeth. "I don't feel anything," he hacked, handing the paraphernalia back to the man.

"It will," the ex- Greek answered. "It takes a while."

A tsunami of nausea passed through Bertrand's abdomen. He stood, thought to himself that he shouldn't have taken that hit, wanted to be in the bathroom, which at least was a normal place of white and cleanliness am I feeling it he thought? He turned to the big, man, the big ugly man and stumbled towards the stairs and said "I'll be right back," he said, trying to right himself and walk like he wasn't feeling anything which led to a sort of stuttered swagger, and he thinks of the Santos's chewing, chew, chew, chew, and marches for a moment until it comes over him, he's smoking baby brains, baby brains, baby brains! He marched to the top of the stairs, feeling each sconce in the hall on his way by and thinking "bathroom, bathroom, bathroom! I need silence and whiteness." It takes forever to get down the hall and up the stairs.

He stumbles through the first door he sees, Bau's door, anyone's door, but "door" is a goal he can focus on, think about, force his will to move towards, and turns the knob, falling through. What a tiny hit, the Bertrand thinks, thinking, "That was such a small hit. A baby hit. Was it baby brains? Where am I?" Is this, he thinks, the bathroom? Why's it so dark, and what happened to the pull cord that used to be here, he gropes for it, twice, and doesn't find it so he thinks he'll walk back to the wall, feel for it slowly, because even though he knows EXACTLY where it is, there's always the off chance that he'll crash into it like a crash test dummy he thinks a crash test dummy ON THE LOOSE with a GOOSE. Where the hell is he?

"You're in my room, Bertrand," says a voice, caring, loving, and he looks up and it's Bau, smiling, naked, glowing yellow in the center of the room, stands on his bed like a structural pillar in the Grand temple of Freemasonry, or Free— manson— ry, because Bau looks like Manson, long beard, no swastika in the head but instead a glowing disc of ultraviolet light, and he's never noticed that before. Wrapped around Bau's legs, Amy, the South African Hooker of Perfection, massages his scarred and bruised and bloodied, too white from never wearing shoes, feet with her long, dark hair, she coats Bau's feet with vanilla scented wax from a crumpled handkerchief, she puts wax on his feet and then rubs it in, it cakes and rolls into works of wax and she picks up the worms, puts them in the handkerchief, where she balls it all up together again and starts anew, an eternal cycle of wax on, wax off.

"So I am in your room," says Bertrand. "I hope I didn't...

interrupt anything. Are you two busy?"

Too busy?

Bau laughs the joyous and loving laugh, the laugh of Adam upon first seeing his newborn son, Cain. "Bertrand, it's nothing you're not welcome to interrupt. Have you met Amy?"

Amy stops rubbing Bau's feet for long enough to say, "We've been introduced."

"Hey, yeah," says Bertrand. "Yeah, she hit me with a car earlier. I got a huge bang on the back of my head. And then she tried to fuck me, but alas, no deal, even though I wanted to more than anything else in the whole damned world. At that time. So now she's pissed. Hey, did I really just smoke baby brains?"

Bau and Amy laugh, and Bertrand begins to count the colors in their mouths. "BABY brains?" asks Amy. "Is Santos up to that again? He's never smoked baby brains!"

"So I didn't just smoke the powdered brains of some dead baby?"

"Bertrand, the brains of a dead baby?" said Bau, wiping his third eye with the mouth on his finger. "That's far too absurd to be true."

"Oh, so he's done this kind of thing before?" Santos, bloated, or just his face floats (drifts) by in the darkness, its Stalin moustache flapping like a hummingbird's wings, a trail of powder blue smoke behind him. "Well that's good to know. I was very worried for a moment. I haven't been having the greatest night, see, and— "

"I know, you poor dear," said Amy. "First hit by a car and then having to meet Santos. Awful! But I'm telling you, he's a big teddy bear. He's like a... like a... fun, Greek, Teddy Roosevelt!"

"Is that who you picture when you fuck him?" asks Bertrand.

Amy glares. "We are close, yes. But no more close than he and Bau."

"Whoa! Stop there." He holds his arm up, palm extended. "Tooo much information. No thanks. Don't need the visual."

Bau's smile extends itself horizontally. "You've had a bit too much, haven't you, man?" He sits, the pillar crumbles to the bed, and extends his arm around Amy as she busily twists her hair into pigtails.

"I think I'm just not used to it, whatever it is. What is it, anyhow, if it's not baby brains?"

"Oh, it's something experimental we're working on."

"Who's working on it?"

"Just us and some friends of ours." Amy answered. "Old friends of ours."

"You know, Bertrand," said Bau, "we're always looking for more people to help out. You ever wonder why it is," he glowed, "that I can live here in this great big house with no income? Or why I'm always buying shit from you two or three at a time instead of in large amounts?"

"I have wondered, yeah." Now that he mentions it, yeah.

"Well, now you know. We're paying Santos to make this stuff. It's a new drug, man, and we're going to put it in the city's water supply. Dig?"

Despite the fact that he's busy comparing Amy to an upright airplane, Bertrand asks, "no, I don't 'dig.' What you're telling me is that I smoked some fucking drug that you're going to use to spike the water supply? What the fuck, man!?"

Bau emits words, from somewhere below his nose but above his beard. "Don't worry, it won't hurt you. You've taken drugs before. It's for the others, the population. General people. You know, your everyday working Eddie who doesn't have a clue or give a shit, who's so trapped in reality it makes you want to vomit. It's to make them see visions. Hallucinate, wake 'em up."

Bertrand fretted. "The hippies have been talking about that forever. There's even an author who— "

"Yeah, but that's acid. This shit ain't acid, man. Acid, that just wakes you up to images, flitterings, picture birds that fly by your windows. All that, that's a level down from consciousness. But this stuff, this drug that you so wonderfully helped us test this evening, this goes a level up. This drug makes you see into the realm of the Ideal. With acid it's what could be. With this it's what it..."

"What it should be," interrupted Amy.

"That's why Santos tells people that were working on something that's made from baby brains. Because when you take it, you start thinking with the brain of a baby. They, those tiny babies, just came from the place this stuff gets you to. Funny, huh?" Bau crossed his arms, lifted his left hand to his chin. "I guess it's working for you? Such a small hit, you say— you'll be down soon."

"A short ride," said Amy.

"And what does he use, then, to make this drug?" asked Bertrand.

Bau and Amy shrugged. "That's why he gets paid so well. He's the only one who knows how. This way, if they ever capture one of us, they, you know..."

"They won't be able to get it out of us," said Amy, kissing Bau's cheek and taking down her hair.

"So whaddaya say, buddy? You in?" Bau eyed him intensely, more intensely than ever before, more intensely than a friend should look at another friend.

Bertrand considered for a moment. He thought to himself that he wasn't feeling the effects of the drug so much anymore. I wonder, he thought, what this drug really is. It's a nice one, that's for sure, but... but it's no nicer than anything else I've done before. A jaded and throaty laugh wandered up from downstairs, Santos's laugh. Before he realized it, a "no" escaped from Bertrand's mouth.

"No?" asked Bau. "You have no interest in changing the world?"

"Nope," answered Bertrand. "You want to know what I think? I think that crazy Greek or non— Greek— no, Greek!— that Greek fucker downstairs is fleecing you two for all you're worth. I think he mixed some coke with some high grade hash and somehow powdered it and dyed it blue, and now he's got you and your little group thinking you're seeing some 'Ideal World.' That's what I think. And that's why the only thing that interests me is taking the piss I came to take in the first place. Where's the bathroom?"

Bau shook his head and sighed. He glanced at Amy, who began to put her underwear on, left leg and then right. "First door on the left, not right."

Bertrand started to walk out to the hall, turned back for a moment. "Guys, I really..." but they were too busy getting dressed to notice him, so he crossed the hall into the bathroom.

He closed the door and it locked behind him. Squinting to make anything out in the dark, he grasped for the light cord he thought he'd been trying for earlier. Still unable to mark its exact position, he groped towards the wall, where he anticipated the jab of the plastic light switch, which would provide him with some orientation. He found the switch and flicked it, once, twice, to no avail. He tried the door, but couldn't figure out how it unlocked. He shouted for help.

* * *

Approximately an hour later, the cold sweats began. Then the flashes of severe abdominal pain. The darkness became empty as he slumped against the wall.

* * *

Some time later, the door opened just long enough to admit a meaty tattooed hand, which tossed something to the floor before exiting, slamming the door, and the echoing click of the key turning in the lock woke Bertrand, who felt that something near his leg. Reaching down slowly, trying to get past the pain, he groped for the object. His hand closed around the crinkled texture of a brown paper bag. Reaching into the bag, Bertrand found a lighter, a small glass pipe, and a quantity of a shimmering, blue, iridescent powder, which he sifted through his fingers as he smiled.

7. Gods and Famous People: An Unfinished Play

SCENE 1: EMPTY STAGE BEFORE CURTAINS. After the incidental music stops, the AUTHOR steps into a spotlight on stage, holding a manuscript under his arm. Clearing his throat, he begins to speak, shielding his eyes from the spotlight.

AUTHOR

(It should seem as if the AUTHOR is not an actor, but indeed the real author. Perhaps, if time allows, a stagehand who is not part of the cast could introduce the author.)

Good evening, ladies and gentlemen. Thank you all for coming, and I hope you didn't give too much to the vultures at the door. I'm the author of this play, and I thought I'd better explain a few things before the show starts. First of all, I should warn you that the play is written in what is called a 'uchronic' format. This means that the production contains elements from many different time periods. This play is not a prisoner of chronological setting. I'd originally intended to set it in the early Twentieth Century, but I changed my mind, just as I intend, of course, to change yours. you see, this play is an exercise in what the communists of the cold war era would have called 'mind control.' I've attempted to construct a reality in which you, as members of the audience, begin to doubt your own. Unfortunately, by limiting myself to one specific modus tempit, or mode of time, it would have been more difficult to maintain a feeling of not— realism, or if you will, meta— realism. As one who values societal judgments on 'reality,' such as the ones made by my wonderful audience, I can respect the need for a venture into the realms of explanation, an apology, as it were — I am fond of that phrase. And so I leave you with this warning, which the wise will apply to the world outside the play as well as the one within it: NOTHING IS EVER WHAT IT SEEMS. Period. Thank you.

(The author bows and exits. After a moment, the curtains open and reveal a single spot on a darkened stage, into which enters the PLAYWRIGHT. He has the same clothing as the AUTHOR, and also

holds what looks like a manuscript
but is actually a newspaper.)

PLAYWRIGHT

Good evening, ladies and gentlemen. I am the
playwright. This play is my work, and my work
alone, done with no collaboration except that of the
muses. Before the show begins, or rather, before we
enter into the plot, I feel it necessary to clarify a few
things.

(He signals to the booth and a
projecting screen is made available to
him. This screen can either be an
overhead projector, on which he
illustrates his points, or a pre— set
slide projector that is changed by his
signal.)

Thank you. Now then. First of all, a word on
chemistry. I would like to remind you that water, a
liquid, is made of two parts hydrogen and one part
oxygen.

(He draws/shows a picture of a water
molecule.)

These are both gases. Hydrogen, the most common element in our universe, is lighter than air. Oxygen, as we all know, is necessary for human respiration. We cannot, however, access oxygen to breathe underwater, nor does water float away.

Next, politics. In theory, communist political systems would not deal with physical wealth and class distinctions. In practice, however, a pseudo bourgeois is formed from the ruling class, and the proletariat has no access

to the ruling class's wealth. Capitalist political systems, on the other hand, hold that no class distinctions will exist in a democratic capitalistic society due to the right of the entire society to vote. However, this does not take into account the phenomenon of voter apathy, which results in a pseudo bourgeois upper class with access to corporate wealth. Ergo, communism and capitalism result in the same social systems. They are two different sides to the same evil coin.

Next, linguistics. Language has a symbolic value that is often socially invalid. For instance, what does the word 'asshole':

(Writing) ASSHOLE

mean? Linguistically, it refers to the rectum, which rids the body of waste. From a teleological standpoint, with which we investigate the philosophical purpose of a thing, the 'asshole' is necessary for the proper function of human health. In the case of the physical asshole, the end truly does justify the means.:

ASSHOLE: NECESSARY FOR HUMAN HEALTH

Now, suppose you were to call your boss an asshole. Would he think it was a compliment? After all, by teleological definition, you've just called him necessary for human health. But, no. Nope. Societal symbolism associates the asshole with the human waste that passes through it:

ASSHOLE = SHIT by ASSOCIATION

This association isn't real. The asshole is not excretory material. Nonetheless, the word takes on a negative value and, well, you'd be fired, see?

Next, semiotics. If you repeat a word often enough, it loses its meaning. Let's try it. Repeat the following word ten times quickly:

GROUP

(He leads the audience in the repetition) By the tenth time, your brain no longer associates the word 'group' with the meaning 'a collection if things'.

Next, metaphysics. The Gnostics, a group of religious thinkers of the Roman Era, believed that the universe was created by a God that is either blind, stupid, or insane, and that, as a consequence, it shares his flaws.:

BLIND, STUPID GOD → BLIND, STUPID REALITY

They also believed, however, that through direct knowledge of this fact, humans can transcend past this Idiot God into the realms of true freedom.

TRUE FREEDOM→BLIND, STUPID GOD→BLIND, STUPID REALITY→HUMAN PERCEIVES! SAVED!

Well, on with the show. I apologize if I've bored you. The rest of the program will be much more interesting. Thank you.

> (The projector disappears and the lights come up on a modern— ish apartment with a chair, a writing desk, and a stereo with CD player. PLAYWRIGHT sits in the chair and begins reading his paper.)

PLAYWRIGHT

Steve should be here any minute now.

> (There is a knock at the door. HE looks up and shakes his head, winking to the audience in a way that implies 'here we go!')

Here he is now!

> (Crossing to door and opening it a crack.)

Hello? Steve?

GIRL

(From outside door.)

Hello? Are you there?

PLAYWRIGHT

(Confused. Aside.)

A girl?

(To door.)

Yes, I'm here. Can I help you?

GIRL

I don't know. I hope so. Can I please come in?

PLAYWRIGHT

Um . . . I don't know. Can I trust you?

GIRL

Yes! Please, I need to talk to you.

PLAYWRIGHT

Do I know you? Did Steve send you?

GIRL

No. At least, I don't think so.

PLAYWRIGHT

Then of course I'll let you in.

(Aside.)

Complete strangers are often more trustworthy than good friends.

(He opens the door. GIRL enters, visibly upset.)

GIRL

Thank you. Thanks. Can I sit down?

PLAYWRIGHT

By all means, go ahead. (SHE does.) Now then. How can I help you?

GIRL

Aren't you going to introduce yourself?

PLAYWRIGHT

Sorry?

GIRL

Who are you? I need to know that you know who
you are.

PLAYWRIGHT

(Working it out.)

You need to know . . . that I know . . . who I am?

GIRL

That's right.

PLAYWRIGHT

Well, I'm the Playwright! I'm also the main character
in this very play.

GIRL

And that's who you are?

PLAYWRIGHT

Yes, it's what I do.

GIRL

That's not an identification. What you do is not who
you are.

PLAYWRIGHT

It can be.

GIRL

No it can't.

PLAYWRIGHT

It is right now. Look! It was a very kind thing I did
opening my door for a complete stranger. You
could've killed me or wanted to rob me of my
personal possessions. You've absolutely no right to
start a philosophical debate on the nature of being
in my play. At least, not yet, anyway.

GIRL

I'm sorry. It's just that . . . that . . .

(Breaking into tears.)

I don't know who I am!

PLAYWRIGHT

I'm sorry, come again?

GIRL

I don't know who I am! I can't remember anything about

myself. It's all gone.

PLAYWRIGHT

Your name?

GIRL

Gone!

PLAYWRIGHT

Your date of birth?

GIRL

Gone!

PLAYWRIGHT

Where did you come from?

GIRL

It's GONE! Gone! I found myself downstairs with nothing but the clothes on my back. The old man in the hall —

PLAYWRIGHT

With the goat?

GIRL

That's him. He told me that you were the playwright and that you might be able to help me find my identity. You must help me!

PLAYWRIGHT

> (Consoling, but obviously
> uncomfortable.)

There, there.

> (He gives her his handkerchief,
> which she uses rather loudly.)

Well, this is a conundrum.

GIRL

How's that?

PLAYWRIGHT

It's just that I don't know who you are either.

GIRL

But you wrote this play, didn't you?

PLAYWRIGHT

I did, but I write from personal experience. I've never seen you before. You're not my friend Steve, whom I was expecting. He had the package that the plot revolves around.

GIRL

Oh, dear. I've ruined your play.

PLAYWRIGHT

Oh, dear indeed. That's all right. Steve's late.

GIRL

What will I do?

PLAYWRIGHT

Calm down. We'll get this sorted out.

GIRL

How?

PLAYWRIGHT

I'm thinking.

(Thinks.)

We can begin by deciding what you're not.

GIRL

Deciding what I'm not? How will that help?

PLAYWRIGHT

If we know what you're not, it will be easier for us to figure out what you are.

GIRL

I guess that makes sense, in a twisted sort of way.

PLAYWRIGHT

So, what aren't you?

GIRL

Let's see.

(Playing along.)

I'm not your friend Steve.

PLAYWRIGHT

One moment.

(Retrieves a clipboard and a pen from
the desk.)

Not Steve.

(Takes note.)

GIRL

And I'm not a Biblical Prophet.

PLAYWRIGHT

Not a Biblical Prophet.

GIRL

Nor am I a gar.

PLAYWRIGHT

Not a gar.

GIRL

Or a perch, for that matter.

PLAYWRIGHT

Isn't a perch a bird?

GIRL

No. It's a fish. Like a gar.

PLAYWRIGHT

A fish like a gar?

GIRL

No. A fish like a gar is a fish.

PLAYWRIGHT

Ah. I was sure it was a bird.

GIRL

No, it's definitely a fish. Or... a post that birds sit on!

PLAYWRIGHT

I think it's safe to say that you're not Steve, a Biblical Prophet, a fish of any kind, a bird, or a device upon which birds rest.

GIRL

This is going nowhere.

PLAYWRIGHT

I think we're making progress. We already have four things that you're not.

GIRL

But there are an infinite number of things that I'm not!

PLAYWRIGHT

On the contrary! You are something. If you are something, then there can't be an infinite number of things that you're not, because infinity includes everything, and that would make you nothing.

GIRL

(Confused.)

I never was very good at math.

PLAYWRIGHT

It's simple. If infinity includes everything, then you are a part of infinity. If you are part of infinity, then everything that you are not is less than infinite, which, by the simple act of reason, leads us to conclude that there are a finite number of things that you are not, because anything less than infinity is finite. You are, quite simply, infinity minus you.

GIRL

Did I mention that this is going nowhere?

PLAYWRIGHT

You're right.

GIRL

Besides, we know I'm a human girl.

PLAYWRIGHT

Hmm. Then it's time for a different approach.

(HE returns to the desk and trades
the clipboard for a phonebook.)

Let's try the phonebook.

GIRL

The phonebook?

PLAYWRIGHT

Yep. We'll go by name. We know you're a girl, so
that should help.

GIRL

The whole thing? That'll take hours!

PLAYWRIGHT

Nonsense! This is a play! The lights will go down for five seconds to denote the passage of time and then come back up and we'll be all the way through.

GIRL

Oh. Okay, then. Let's give it a try.

PLAYWRIGHT

Right. We'll start with the first girl. 'Miriam B. Aartwyk.' Is she you?

GIRL

No.

PLAYWRIGHT

Fine. 'Susan Abacabie?'

GIRL

Nope.

> (The lights dim for five seconds and
> then come back up.)

PLAYWRIGHT

'Zelda Z. Zebrovski?'

GIRL

No, that's not it. Go on.

PLAYWRIGHT

That's it. That's all.

GIRL

That's horrible. If I'm not in the phonebook, then I
must not exist.

PLAYWRIGHT

Ah, but you could be unlisted.

GIRL

I guess I could, couldn't I? But what now? We have

no more options.

PLAYWRIGHT

There are always options!

GIRL

WHAT? What can we do?

(SHE begins to sob again.)

PLAYWRIGHT

Oh, dear. Calm down, please. We'll work this out.
We have to.

GIRL

We have to?

PLAYWRIGHT

If we don't, and Steve doesn't show, there's no plot
resolution.

GIRL

Good point. Unless this is a tragedy! Is this a
tragedy?

PLAYWRIGHT

I forget. I wrote it so long ago.

> (After a moment of thinking, he
> snaps his fingers.)

Ah ha!

GIRL

What?

PLAYWRIGHT

Hypnosis.

GIRL

Hypnosis?

PLAYWRIGHT

Yes, hypnosis. Simple hypnotic regression.

GIRL

Are you a hypnotist?

PLAYWRIGHT

(Huffy.)

I am a playwright!

GIRL

Oh.

PLAYWRIGHT

We can hypnotize you right now. Just make yourself comfortable.

> (HE rummages through a desk drawer and, from underneath a pile of odd items, removes a pocket-watch. Sorting through his CD collection, he removes Debussy's "Prelude d'un
>
> Apres- midi d'un Faune" and places it in the CD player, starting the music.)

GIRL

Lovely!

PLAYWRIGHT

What's that?

GIRL

This music.

PLAYWRIGHT

Ah, yes. It's the "Prelude to the afternoon of a faun," by Claude Debussy.

GIRL

I like it. What should I do?

PLAYWRIGHT

Like I said, make yourself comfortable. Relax.

> (Crossing to GIRL, he begins to hypnotize her in the traditional fashion, using the watch as a pendulum.)

Relax. Listen to the music. Imagine lush green fields where rows and rows of wildflowers wave in time with the instruments. All is calm and peaceful and you're falling into a deep, deep sleep. Deeper. Deeper, like you're falling backwards into a deep, deep, dark place. Deep. Deep. Back.

> (She falls asleep.) (Aside.)

As the Playwright, I knew this would work.

> (To GIRL.)

Can you hear me?

GIRL

(In a hypnotic trance.)

I can.

PLAYWRIGHT

Now then —

(Quite unexpectedly, the door slams open. A man, frantic, in the dress of a Nineteenth Century gentlemen with wide— brimmed hat and red cape dashes in. He is bespectacled and his cape is muddied. To the PLAYWRIGHT's surprise, the man closes and locks the door. He is CLAUDE DEBUSSY, famous composer. He barricades the door with a chair and stands, out of breath.)

PLAYWRIGHT

(Without looking up.)

Steve?

DEBUSSY

(Loud)

Help help help!!!

PLAYWRIGHT

Steve, would you please be quiet? I am attempting an experiment in hypnotism!

DEBUSSY

Sorry!

PLAYWRIGHT

(Looks up)

You're not Steve. Who the hell are you?

DEBUSSY

I am the great composer Claude Debussy. You must help me!

PLAYWRIGHT

You, too, huh? Help you how?

DEBUSSY

I must hide!

PLAYWRIGHT

From who?

DEBUSSY

There is a wild man after me!

PLAYWRIGHT

That doesn't give you any right to come bursting
into my room.

DEBUSSY

If you are a good man, you will give me shelter. I fear
for my life!

PLAYWRIGHT

Fine! Just be quiet. This girl is in a hypnotic trance,
through which we seek to learn her ide— did you
say you're Claude Debussy?

DEBUSSY

I did.

PLAYWRIGHT

Wow! Listen!

> (He crosses to the CD player and
> restarts the "Prelude".)

It's you! This is your "Prelude!"

DEBUSSY

What?

PLAYWRIGHT

Yes, listen! It's being played on a compact disc,
which uses a small beam of light to play reproduced
music. Since you're from the Nineteenth Century,
you must be fascinated by our modern technology.

> (DEBUSSY crosses slowly to the CD
> player, listening. He stares at the
> speaker, shakes it.)

DEBUSSY

This is appalling!

PLAYWRIGHT

What?

DEBUSSY

I didn't write this drivel.

PLAYWRIGHT

Huh?

DEBUSSY

I didn't write this. Surely this is the invention of some cheap imitator of your time, and it is loosely based on my Prelude.

PLAYWRIGHT

No, this is yours. Don't you recognize?

DEBUSSY

I will agree that it carries the same basic melody as my Prelude, but this is not what I composed.

PLAYWRIGHT

(Crosses to CD player and removes
the case to the CD.)

Look. It says right here. "Prelude d'un Apres-midi
d'un Faune" by Claude Debussy.

DEBUSSY

Slander!

PLAYWRIGHT

How can you say that you didn't write this?

DEBUSSY

To begin with, the tempo is all wrong. Also, it is
much too allegro. And the flutes are not bright
enough. And where are my beautiful triplets? This is
'dah dah dah dah dah,' not 'dah dah dah, dah dah
dah.' No. I did not write this drivel.

PLAYWRIGHT

Well.

DEBUSSY

Not a bad try, though. A decent imitation. Shouldn't

you be attending to your hypnotized girl?

PLAYWRIGHT

Oops. You're right.

DEBUSSY

Do you have any beer?

PLAYWRIGHT

We're not so frightened of the wild man any more,
are we?

DEBUSSY

Bad imitation shocked me out of it. Do you?

PLAYWRIGHT

Sure. It's in the kitchen. Help yourself.

DEBUSSY

Thanks.

    (DEBUSSY exits to the kitchen.)

(PLAYWRIGHT turns back to the
GIRL.)

PLAYWRIGHT

Now then. Can you hear me?

GIRL

Yes.

PLAYWRIGHT

Good. Now I want you to remember. Go back . . . go
back . . . can you see anything?

GIRL

I see . . . I see a brown haze.

PLAYWRIGHT

Concentrate on the haze. Make it as real as you can.
What is happening?

GIRL

It's a desk. It's a desk, I think.

153

PLAYWRIGHT

A desk? Where is the desk?

GIRL

I don't know. There's a big empty room. Many things . . . and papers.

(DEBUSSY enters from kitchen with a beer and a sandwich.)

DEBUSSY

Now. Why are we doing this?

PLAYWRIGHT

She's got amnesia. She can't remember who she is.

DEBUSSY

Can I try? I've done this before.

PLAYWRIGHT

Done it before?

DEBUSSY

Sure!

PLAYWRIGHT

Oh, okay. We'll see if you can get anything out of
her.

DEBUSSY

Thanks!

> (Crossing to the GIRL and leaning in
> close.)

Girl, this is Debussy. I am a composer. Can you hear
me?

GIRL

Yes.

DEBUSSY

Good. Listen very closely. When you awaken,
whenever you hear the word "bullfighting," you will
bark like a dog.

PLAYWRIGHT

Hey!

DEBUSSY

SHHH! Wake up!

> (He quickly hands his drink and
> sandwich to PLAYWRIGHT and claps
> his hands. GIRL wakes up and rubs
> her eyes.)

PLAYWRIGHT

(To DEBUSSY.)

You asshole!

DEBUSSY

I am essential to human health!

PLAYWRIGHT

Why'd you do that?

DEBUSSY

(Taking back his food and drink.)

I saw it done in a parlour once in Paris. I wanted to
see if it would really work.

PLAYWRIGHT

You said you'd done it before!

DEBUSSY

Seen it done, yes.

GIRL

What happened?

PLAYWRIGHT

We were doing just fine until the 'great composer' here decided to goof around with your subconscious.

GIRL

(Noticing DEBUSSY.)

Oh! And you are . . .

DEBUSSY

(Wiping his hand on his cape and offering it to GIRL.)

The Great Claude Debussy!

(He bows and GIRL stands.)

GIRL

Oh, then you wrote this beautiful piece that we're listening to?

DEBUSSY

Madame, that insinuation is slanderous and all I have to say in response is bullfighting.

(GIRL barks.)

PLAYWRIGHT

Dear Lord!

GIRL

What?

PLAYWRIGHT

(Uncomfortably.)

Nothing. You remembered a desk.

GIRL

I did! And there were papers on it! With a name on the papers!

PLAYWRIGHT

Do you remember the name?

GIRL

(Struggling to think.)

No.

DEBUSSY

Was it... bullfighting?

(GIRL barks.)

PLAYWRIGHT

(To DEBUSSY.)

Would you please stop that?

DEBUSSY

Of course. I mean, how often does one really hear

the word bullfighting?

(GIRL barks.)

She'll probably never hear the word again.

PLAYWRIGHT

She'd better not. Or else I'll turn you out to your

wild man.

DEBUSSY

(Actually nervous.)

I don't really think you'd do that.

PLAYWRIGHT

Try me.

GIRL

What are you two talking about?

PLAYWRIGHT and DEBUSSY

Nothing.

GIRL

Oh. You have beer?

DEBUSSY

In the kitchen. There is a box of cold air wherein rests the beer.

PLAYWRIGHT

The refrigerator.

DEBUSSY

Hmm?

PLAYWRIGHT

The box of cold air. That's what it's called.

DEBUSSY

Okay. I know.

> (He shrugs as if PLAYWRIGHT is an idiot.)

GIRL

Can I have a beer?

PLAYWRIGHT

Help yourself.

GIRL

Thanks.

> (Exits to kitchen.)

DEBUSSY

Well, what now?

PLAYWRIGHT

I was expecting my friend Steve to come by with a very important package. But he's very late. So now I've got to help this poor girl remember who she is.

DEBUSSY

Do you find her, heh heh,

>(making an illicit gesture)

attractive?

PLAYWRIGHT

Come on. She's my creation. Don't be silly.

DEBUSSY

Sorry. Why has she forgotten who she is?

PLAYWRIGHT

I don't know.

DEBUSSY

You know what I'd do?

PLAYWRIGHT

(Suspicious.)

I don't know. You've already offered to help once.

DEBUSSY

No, really. When I lose something, I trace my steps. Backtrack. You know, I go back over everything I did before I lost it.

PLAYWRIGHT

This isn't about a set of keys, here.

DEBUSSY

Of course not! Still, take her to the park.

PLAYWRIGHT

To the park?

DEBUSSY

Absolutely. Think about it. People, nature, reality in its varied forms. Plus, she had to get here somehow, didn't she? The park is right outside your house. Maybe if she sees the outside she'll have some recollection of how she got here and can follow a path back.

PLAYWRIGHT

The park, huh?

DEBUSSY

I was just out on such a stroll, actually.

PLAYWRIGHT

Yeah, but you were attacked by a wild man.

(GIRL enters from kitchen.)

GIRL

You were out of beer, so I made some tea.

DEBUSSY

Did I take the last one? I'm sorry.

PLAYWRIGHT

That's all right.

(To GIRL.)

Mr. Debussy suggested we go for a walk.

GIRL

A walk? To where?

PLAYWRIGHT

How about the park across the street? You had to get here somehow. Maybe you'll recognize something.

GIRL

Okay. We'll go for a walk. Will you join us, Mr. Debussy?

DEBUSSY

(Nervous laugh.)

No, no. I think I'll just stay here.

PLAYWRIGHT

(Taking down barricade and unlocking door.)

He's hiding from a wild man.

GIRL

Oh! I'm sorry. I didn't realize —

DEBUSSY

No, no. That's all right. Quite characteristic of the day I've been having, actually. If it's not a problem, I'll just stay here until you get back.

PLAYWRIGHT

Certainly. You can let Steve in if he stops by. Just don't break anything.

GIRL

I love your music!

DEBUSSY

(Mutters something unintelligible.)

PLAYWRIGHT

What was that?

DEBUSSY

I said, bullfighting!

(GIRL barks, lights dim, and curtains fall.)

8. Note Found on a Red Velvet Chair

This morning, upon waking, I noticed that someone had placed a new sculpture in the courtyard outside. I can see it through the window, the dirty window that reminds me of Her mascara covered cheeks, streaks of dull black carried down the smooth surface by tears, or rain. I'd like to go look at the pyramid, investigate how it got there, but there are simply too many things between my red velvet chair and the pyramid, like Zeno's paradox. You know, in order to get from A to B, you first have to get halfway there, to point C, but to get to point C, you'll first have to get halfway there, to point D, ad infinitum, so you can never reach B, such a chore, and I'm so comfortable here in my chair.

You see, in order for me to get to that pyramid, which seems to consist of marble blocks, white— and I can tell they're white because through the blackened, streaked, window they're grey, except for the places where they're broken by a dull green, perhaps a serpent or an eel, molded from stained copper, that eternally climbs to the summit of the pyramid— in order for me to get to the pyramid, the first thing I have to do is to get halfway there.

Based on my estimate, made via my meagre knowledge of geometry and triangles and shadows, the halfway point between my chair and the pyramid is roughly twelve feet.

Twelve feet away, someone has planted another sculpture, Rodin- like, or Muñoz, a woman of bronze, black and wrinkled, wilted, a sculpture of solidified tissue paper, shriveled, eternally screaming. The woman is covered in dust; I estimate that there are approximately seven million, seven hundred and thirty- four thousand, three hundred and sixteen specks of dust on the statue, enough to turn its color from a dull bronze to a dull iron- grey. That number, by the way, in case you need to see it as a number, is 7,743,316.

This dust consists of an entire civilisation built on filth, with mites as citizens and skin flecks as buildings, and dust its earth, and its art is excrement. Any society is based on what its members are able to produce, and excrement is all that mites can produce, so the basis for mite culture, for mite politics, for mite art, must be excrement. The sculpture- woman seems to scream vividly, and one can imagine the terror of her scream, but if she were real and were to scream, or to move at all, a great, vast, cloud- city of dust mites would launch into the air before her, doomed forever to wander the atmosphere of the courtyard, each breath taken by a visitor to the courtyard would invite the remnants of this mite society into his or her lungs, into his or her hair, into his or her clothing and eyes and skin.

Perhaps this is why she's screaming: the horror of being covered in a society of crawling, excrement— producing mites, but anything she could do to remove the mites or even to move a foot to the left or right would launch the mites into the air where they would infest someone anew, and soon the mites would spread in clouds over the world, so the lady chose instead, halfway through her scream, to freeze into a sculpture, her final realization, to transubstantiate herself into a bronze sculpture in order to save us from the mites. She has become the Saviour of Man in this respect; her decision to freeze in passivity so as not to launch the mites into the air was the greatest and most terrible sacrifice she could have made, and she screams forever, silently, while the mites, helpless but perfect symbols of the sins of man, thrive on her eternally frozen form, producing sculptures of their own out of excrement.

This is, of course, all conjectural, because in order for me to truly investigate this sculpture, I'd have to move twelve feet, which means I'd first have to move halfway there, six feet, and make my way past the carven door, six feet away, as I mentioned. The door, while indifferent to my decision to open or close it, nonetheless remains heavier than any other door, as it contains the entire range of human potentiality; it depicts the entire range of human doors. Carved into its cedar surface, the branches and leaves which used to cover cave entries for camouflage on the darkest primitive nights strut jaggedly up and down the sides, while the deerskin flap of the hunter's hut flows wave- like across the top panel. An intricate fiber curtain dances in wood over the flap, upon which rests, unobtrusive, a simple wooden plank, undoubtedly unhinged, surrounded by another wooden door, this one with hinges, itself surrounding a great bronze Romanesque door depicting Janus, the Roman God of Doorways between a myriad of multi- hued Corinthian columns.

In his left hand, Janus holds another wooden door, this one carved to represent the Medieval conception of the ascent of the soul to heaven, or its descent to hell, the figures thick and stocky, peasants perhaps, semi- realistic, crawling down tunnels of fire, lapped at by naked and horrific insectoid demon wasps with stingers of steel, and heaven sucks up other figures in beams of light and saints. In his other hand, Janus holds an airlock, round, blue, separating alien- suited men from what could be either water, speckled with fish, or the vastness of space, speckled with stars. The men rest contentedly in a tube of silver, praising the door in Latin,

"Holy art thou, O Door, our protector, thou keepest us safe from that which is outside," except for one man, helmeted, face visible through glass and on the other side of the door drifting through the vague sea towards the heaven depicted on the other door, carved eyes gazing up at the Throne of God, a bright yellow- white halo stained with golden shimmering angelic faces, and seated on the Throne, at the very top of the door, is a depiction of the Door to end all Doors, the Alpha door, open on creation, and the Omega door, closed at the end of time, both of which are carved to depict the door which sits six feet away from me, the door that prevents me from investigating the statue of the woman on which the dust mites have built a civilisation of their own, no doubt with their own doors made of excrement.

It's a moot point, really; this collection of carven images remains completely inaccessible to me. Do you realize how far away it is, what lengths I must endure to get from the relative comfort of my red velvet chair to the multifaceted and intricately detailed face of the great door? It's a full six feet away. In order to walk six feet from here, I'd first have to get three feet away from my chair, at which point I'd reach Her body.

I just noticed that there are people surrounding the pyramid in the courtyard. Five or six men, it seems, who all wear standard issue Union Army uniforms, blue, silver buttons like stars of glitter sparkling on their chests. They're methodically combing the ground around the pyramid. The one who seems to be the leader of the men leans over, wipes a single finger over one of the bricks, opens a sack and sprinkles more dust over the sculpture, doing I don't know what. The other men spread out among the courtyard, one sitting on the rim of the fountain to the left of the pyramid, another pausing for a moment to pluck an infinitely detailed mango from the tree to the right of it, scrutinizing the mango, not stopping, as he should, to count the spots on the mango's skin, brushing off a wandering ant, and removing a knife from his pocket. He peels the mango tenderly, softly, as if he is peeling a woman's breast, and the other men continue through their motions, their investigations, searching for something, again coming sometimes between the statue of the woman covered in dust and the pyramid.

I'd like to go and talk to them, ask them what they're doing in my courtyard, but they're so far away from me, I don't think I could make it. I'd have to get to the great, carved door first, infinitely far away, and between me and the door, three feet away from the comfort of my red velvet chair, I'd have to somehow traverse the remnants of a human universe, the entire human experience, the thoughts, feelings, emotions of Her psyche, Her protests and Her agony. Her twisted form, between the mascara stained cheeks that look like my window, wears a smirk on its face that I assume can only mean that she lived Her life to the fullest satisfaction, that when I delivered the blade into the mail slot of Her ribs, she had prepared Herself for the moment, and, content, satisfied, mocks me in death, Her half- smile contrasting vividly with the frozen shriek on the bronze sculpture outside.

She is a universe. Contained in Her form are the myriad experiences of Her life, Her introduction to me at Antonio's soirée, and our eventual courtship, Her acceptance of my engagement ring, which decorates Her finger like a miniature diamond tiara. Within Her form, there on the tiles between my chair and the door, another society thrives, produces, and I have released it into the world; it seeps out of the wound in Her abdomen and grows, expands, mingling with the dust, microcosmic cities, shadow plays of experience.

The men outside have somehow reached the statue of the screaming woman, and I'm not sure how they were able to cross such a vast and incomprehensible distance. To my chagrin, they are defeating the *raison d'etre* of the statue, dusting it with feathers, the clouds of dust shooting into the atmosphere like sparks from a blacksmith's anvil, perhaps the anvil on which my knife was hammered, the archetypal anvil of God, the God of Doors, who crafts the metal frames of airlocks and the sparks thrown off become societies of mites who sculpt screaming women in excrement. The men in uniform destroy the Saviour of Man with each brush of the feather against bronze, defeat the woman's original intention, and doom us all to a world in which cities of microscopic insects navigate the atmosphere, air the outside of their vehicles, a populated zeppelin in reverse.

Again I contemplate the great abyss of distance between myself and the door, each of Her fingers a galaxy of experiences, every touch recorded there in the flesh between the ridges of Her fingerprints, each caress living and breathing there on the tiles. I live there, too; or at least, my shadow lives there, my form, in Her caresses, as does Antonio's. We both take up residence there, in that infinite space, which I did not realize was infinite until it was too late, until I had already reached into Her galaxy of experience and grabbed for as many stars as possible, thinking that if I pulled them out on the tip of my knife, Her universe would finally end, and I would be the new God of Doors, who dispenses justice to those who would betray others. But, in an infinite universe, you can take away as many stars as you wish without causing even the slightest difference. Instead, Her universe thrives there, captured on the floor, billions of years passing by each second, every letter in every book she's read marching out of Her in intricate formation. How many times did she see the entire alphabet in Her life? Did the alphabet, each time she read it, make extra words for Her out of the words she read? Did she see new words in the sentences she read, the paragraphs, that instructed Her and shaped Her? When she read the word 'shape,' did Her mind take the 'she' out?

Upon further thought, I should be thankful for Her unfaithfulness. Had she not let Antonio into Her universe, I would not have finally had the clock— shaped blinders removed from my eyes; I would not have known what the plurality of the universe

173

truly looks like. Had she not let Antonio into Her universe, I would have remained content, I would have been able still to cross the distances between myself and the pyramid, and I'd know exactly what the copper streak represents. I'd still be content to imagine the universe as limited, to imagine the universe unable to accept both Antonio and myself. But now, since I preserved Her universe, since I created a new universe from Her, on the floor between my chair and the cedar door, I know the truth, I know the actual size of the universe that I created, and I know that no one but a universe's creator can ever take the time to know that universe, as I knew Her before she blossomed, before the cosmos blossomed on my tile floor.

A scritching and knocking at the door tells me that my friends from the courtyard have traversed another six feet, that they have reached the door. Their voices, multifaceted and jellied, somehow reach my ears across the aeons between us, and the door, the Omega door, swings open, and they stand, staring across the abyss, the doorway a scenic overlook onto Her universe, and they step off into the void, but it's futile. And they yell to me, their voices tinny and small, mouse like, the screams of dust mites, by the time they reach my ears. The six men set adrift, floating, in a cosmos of unknowable length, traversing the universe between the door and Her body, trying to reach me, no doubt, to dispense their own justice. I can only smile; I am not afraid. They are three feet away. They'll never reach me.

ABOUT THE AUTHOR

Jeremy Puma was born on the dark side of Saturn's moon Io, in a shack made of pewter. At the age of eight, he received a vision of the failure of the impending Mayan Apocalypse and the emergence of a new world religion based on Manchego cheese. After a dubious exploration of various mysterious undersea realms and a battle with Triton, Lord of the Sunken Cities of Varula, he emerged victorious into a world that he never made.

Jeremy Puma writes nonfiction for people interested in no-nonsense Gnostic spirituality, and fiction of the 'science' and 'weird' varieties. He is the founder-- and only current employee-- of Strange Animal Publications. His literary influences include Philip K. Dick, Julio Cortazar, Kenneth Patchen, Douglas Adams (and their ilk-- isn't "ilk" a great word?).

Jeremy currently resides in Seattle, Washington. He has a beautiful wife, whom he adores, a giggly little son, and two insane dogs. He is available for speaking engagements, complimentary meals, and children's parties.

For more information, please visit www.strangeanimal.net

3291112R00096

Printed in Great Britain
by Amazon.co.uk, Ltd.,
Marston Gate.